THEY CALL ME
AWOL·····

A NOVEL BY
·························

BOB HOSTETLER

HORIZON BOOKS
Camp Hill, Pennsylvania

They Call Me AWOL

To my wife

Robin

Horizon Books
3825 Hartzdale Drive
Camp Hill, PA 17011

ISBN: 0-88965-113-2
LOC Catalog Card Number: 94-68024
© 1994 by Bob Hostetler
Printed in the United States of America

94 95 96 97 98   5   4   3   2   1

Chapter 1

$\mathcal{B}$en Howard yanked up his jacket collar before climbing out of the car. The rain ran down his neck anyway.

"See ya, Dad," he mumbled, as he closed the door and stood back from the sputtering vehicle. He watched, motionless, as his father's decrepit Dodge disappeared down the school driveway. Then, with another yank on his collar, he followed the path the tires had made in the rain-slicked road, walking away from Verona High School.

When he reached the end of the driveway that marked the entrance to the school grounds, he cast a glance behind him at the students sloshing through the rain in the opposite direction. Then quickly turning, he folded his arms, hunched his shoulders against the chilling rain and started the two-mile walk toward home.

"Hey, 'AWOL'," shouted Charlie Parker. Ben looked up through the rain and saw Charlie crossing the street in the distance. Charlie lived with his grandmother in the same trailer park as Ben; he was one of the few friends Ben had at Verona High.

"Skipping school again, AWOL?" said Charlie as he poked Ben in the ribs.

Ben had been tagged "AWOL" (Absent Without Leave) by a freshman biology teacher who would call his name in class and add the comment, "Ben Howard, AWOL again." That had been almost two years ago, and Ben had flunked all but one of his classes during that time.

"Yeah, you know me, Charlie," Ben said. "I got better things to do than listen to Mr. Henson talk about hormones."

"I know, I know, but you're gonna be forty-five and still taking freshman English."

"Naah," said Ben, smacking the side of Charlie's head with his palm. "Don't worry about me. I know what I'm doing."

"Yeah? Well, right now you're makin' me late." Charlie shifted his books to his other hand. "See ya later."

Charlie trotted off toward school. Ben turned and resumed walking away from school, facing into the rain again. After only a few steps, Ben heard the homeroom bell ring. In spite of the rain, he smiled. *Charlie's late again.*

Ben thought about his words with Charlie. Charlie was right. If he kept going this way, he'd be a forty-five-year-old high school freshman. Or worse yet, he'd never finish high school and end up a bum on the streets. But for some reason, he just couldn't bring himself to go to school. It wasn't that he was stupid or anything like that. He just couldn't get interested in school.

His father knew he was having trouble in school, but he didn't know Ben had seldom attended a class in two years. Ben took care of that with doctored report cards and convincing absence excuses. His father figured that Ben was still struggling with his mother's death from cancer almost three years earlier. *That's not it*, Ben thought. *I just hate school. Of course*, he admitted, *as long as Dad thinks that, he'll go a little easier on me.*

Ben had reached the railroad crossing on Reading Road. The trailer court where he lived was on Reading Road, but Ben never walked straight home from here. He was always afraid that his father would pass him coming to or from the trailer since he sometimes returned home after dropping Ben off at school. Instead, Ben followed the railroad tracks, balancing playfully on the slippery rails. The tracks eventually led to within a few hundred yards of his trailer court.

Ben ambled along the tracks until he reached a rise in the landscape that overlooked the trailer court. From this position, he could squat and peer through the trees to see his own trailer, Lot #67, and—most importantly—the driveway where his father's car would be parked if he was home.

Ben crouched low in the mud and leaned forward to see through the clearing in the trees.

"Rats!" he said, biting his fingernail as he spoke. A delivery truck of some kind blocked his view. There was no way to tell for sure whether or not the coast was clear. Should he wait? There was no way to tell how long the truck might be there. Should he look for shelter close by and come back in a half hour? Would the truck be gone by then? He studied the situation pensively.

Finally, Ben made his decision.

"Here goes," he said aloud, as he started down the path he had made through the patch of woods between the tracks and the trailer court.

"If any of the neighbors catch me sneaking between trailers," he said, "I'm a dead duck."

He calculated that if he could get to Lot #70 (which was across the drive and two trailers down from his), he could probably peek under the trailers to see whether or not the car was there.

He entered the trailer park through a hole he and Charlie had created in the wire mesh fence. He stood for a minute to think.

If I step out into the drive, there's always the chance that Dad will be getting in or out of the car at just that moment and he might see me. But it's either that or I get down on my belly and crawl under the trailers. Ben took a deep breath and decided, *I may be crazy, but I'm not that crazy.*

But just as Ben started to step out into the drive at the corner of the trailer where he stood, the trailer door swung open. Ben dropped to his belly and rolled under the trailer. He held his breath as he watched a pair of slippers descend the steps. A hand stretched down and picked up the newspaper in a plastic wrapper. Ben exhaled as the owner of the newspaper and the slippers entered the trailer again and closed the door.

Ben looked down at his muddy clothes. "So much for staying dry," he whispered. He half-rolled, half-crawled to the other side of the trailer, peeked out to be sure no one was there and then ran, hunched, to the next trailer. He repeated that exercise twice, until he arrived at the trailer with "70" painted on the corner. Kneeling in the grass under the numbers, he spied his driveway. It was empty.

"Phew," Ben said. Still being careful not to be seen, he stood up and walked briskly to his trailer. Once inside the door, he kicked his shoes off and left them there. He proceeded, dripping wet and muddy, into his bedroom and shut the door behind him. He tossed his wet clothes into the corner, pulled on a pair of sweatpants and collapsed onto his unmade bed.

Ben had just drifted into a fuzzy sleep when he awoke abruptly. Not sure of what had awakened him, he lay still, with his eyes open.

Suddenly, he heard feet on the steps and a key in the door. Frantically, but as quietly as he could manage, he knelt in his bed to look out the window. His father's car was in the driveway! He slid back into the bed and cast a frenzied glance at his bedroom door. It was closed.

Oh, man, Ben thought. *I'm nailed now.* His father was in the trailer now. Ben could hear every move he made through the thin walls of the mobile home. He approached Ben's door, but went by without pausing. Ben listened breathlessly as his father opened a drawer. He heard him rustling some papers and then his footsteps sounded loud as he passed Ben's room again and went into the living room.

He doesn't know I'm here. Ben lay rigid on his bed, struggling to control the noise of his breathing and the impossibly loud drumming of his heart.

He heard the sound of the phone being lifted from its cradle and the punch punch of his father pushing the numbers. He bit his lip as he listened to the muffled sound of the conversation.

He's calling his appointments, Ben reasoned. *That's why he came back. He didn't come back because of me, he's just making some sales calls in the area and he's phoning them first.*

Ben felt a wave of relief rush over him. He relaxed slightly on the bed, but still didn't change position for fear that his bed might bump the wall and alert his father.

Then, suddenly, panic gripped him again. *My shoes! I left my shoes by the door!* His throat tightened.

If he sees those shoes, he's gonna know. Ben's mind whirred. There was nothing he could do. There was no way to get the shoes now and, anyway, any movement he made in this paper house would announce his presence to his dad. There was nothing to do but sweat and wait for him to notice the muddy shoes by the door.

Ben heard his father hang up. He waited. *What's he doing?* he wondered. He wasn't punching another number. He hadn't moved from his chair by the phone. *He's looking at my shoes,* Ben imagined. *He's seen them!*

As the painful silence lingered, Ben moved his lips soundlessly. *Oh, God,* he mimed. *God, please don't let him see the shoes. Please. Please. I promise I'll go back to school. I know You want me to and I really want to, so please don't let him see the shoes.*

Ben's pleading was interrupted by the sound of the phone buttons being pushed again.

Oh, thank You, thank You. Ben prayed silently, interspersing an occasional *Please, God, please don't let him see the shoes,* hoping to hold God's attention until the crisis passed.

Finally, Ben heard his father utter a deep "goodbye," heard him rise from the chair, shuffle some papers and march again toward his bedroom door. But again he paused. He stayed for a moment in his room at the end of the trailer and then walked to the front door, opened it, locked it and closed it behind him.

Ben lay motionless. The Dodge coughed out of the driveway, and Ben listened as the noise of the engine grew distant. After a few moments of silence, he cautiously inched up to the window above his bed and drew the curtain back slowly. He peeked out. The car was gone.

Determined not to relax yet, Ben crept out of his room. He crossed the living room to the bay windows in the kitchen. Carefully moving the curtains, he gazed up the drive his father's car had just traveled. Finally, convinced that it was safe now, he went to the door and stooped to pick up his shoes. He carried them to his room and pitched them onto the muddy clothes piled in the corner.

He flung himself onto the rumpled bed once more and buried his face into his pillow.

"I'm *definitely* going back to school on Monday," he said.

Chapter 2

$\mathcal{B}$en loved Sundays for many reasons and not only because they broke the monotony of skipping school. This Sunday was no different. As soon as his eyes opened from sleep, his thoughts turned to Randi White. He would be seeing her today.

He walked to the phone and carefully pressed the seven digits that made up Randi's number.

"Hello?"

Ben cleared his throat quickly. "Uh, hello, Pastor White. Is, uh . . . may I speak to Randi?" Ben kicked himself mentally. He always stumbled nervously when he spoke to Randi's father.

"Hold on just a moment, Ben. I'll see if she can come to the phone." Pastor White didn't sound impressed. He never sounded impressed.

"Hi, Ben." It was Randi.

"Hi." *She sounds as gorgeous as she looks*, Ben thought. Sixteen-year-old Randi was the prettiest and most popular girl at church. Even though she and Ben had been "dating" for more than a year now, Ben still had trouble believing she really liked him.

"Is your dad mad at me for calling you this early?"

"No, he's okay," Randi answered.

"We gonna get to spend any time alone today?"

"I don't know, Ben. You know how Sundays are."

"What about . . ."

"Ben," Randi interrupted. "Ben, I gotta go. Everybody's waiting for me at breakfast."

"Okay. See you in church."

As he hung up the receiver, Ben heard his father start his shower. Ben ate a bowl of cold cereal. When his father appeared in the kitchen, Ben left the room to shower and dress for church.

The fifteen-mile drive to church passed in silence. Ben and his father didn't mind talking to each other; they simply hadn't done much of it since Ben's mom had died.

As Ben and his dad pulled into the parking lot of Crestview Community Church, Randi met them. She flashed a wide smile at Ben as he climbed from the car.

"Hi, Mr. Howard," she said, waving slightly.

"I won't be in your class this morning," she said to Ben, lightly grasping his arm as she fell into step beside him. Ben switched his Bible and Sunday school materials to the opposite hand. "I have to help in the primary class. Brenda called in sick right after we hung up."

They stopped inside the double doors of the church as people swarmed around them.

"I'll, uh . . . I'll ask Stefanie to take attendance," Ben said.

"Okay." Randi squeezed his hand. "See ya." They separated.

Ben hurried to the junior high class which he taught. He'd only been teaching this class for a few weeks since the beginning of September. Randi had been the teacher before that, but one Saturday night they were together at her house and she was preparing for the class. Randi suggested they work on it together and before Ben knew what was happening, *he* was teaching and Randi was helping *him*.

He surveyed the circle of students that made up his class. Bobby and Theo squirmed in their chairs, but Gabe, Chuck, Marsha, Brenda, Gina and Stefanie blinked expectantly at him as he opened his reference Bible on his lap. They reminded him of fragile nestlings waiting for food from their mother bird.

After a moment of awkwardness, Ben assigned the attendance book to Stefanie and bowed his head deliberately. Without a word, the other heads in the class bowed, too, and Ben prayed. The lesson proceeded fairly well from that point, but as his students filed out of class, Ben told himself that he could have done a better job if he could have stopped thinking about Randi.

He was jerked back to reality by the strains of the organ vibrating from the sanctuary.

Oh, no, he thought with a sigh, *if the choir's already in, I'm in trouble.*

He quick-stepped his way to the side entrance the choir used just as the sopranos shuffled into the sanctuary. Ben fell in step with them, climbed through the basses and took his place in the tenor section, managing all the while to avoid Mr. Baldoni's annoyed glare. As the choir waited for the organ prelude to stop, Ben fixed his gaze on the back of Randi's head until she turned and offered him a smile.

Ben again had trouble keeping his attention focused.

She's wearing a new dress today, he thought. *At least,*
"All hail the power of Jesus' name . . ."
I think it's new. I wonder if she bought it because—
"Our Father, Who art in heaven . . ."
she thought I'd like it.
"Please turn in your hymnals . . ."
Man, Ben thought, *how do people in love accomplish anything?*
"Our Scripture reading for this morning . . ."
I mean, I can't concentrate. I can't think of anything—
"Will the ushers please come forward?"
but her.
"Lucille will bring a vocal selection entitled . . ."
I can't believe how this morning has gone. It's like—
"Let us pray. . . ."
we never get to see each other anymore.
"My sermon this morning . . ."
Maybe this afternoon . . . maybe. If I can have lunch—
"And in conclusion . . ."
at Todd's house. I can walk over to Randi's—
"Rise and sing our closing hymn. . . ."
for part of the afternoon. That's it!
"Amen."
That's it! I gotta find Todd. Where's Todd, for crying out loud? At last Ben spotted his friend Todd. He vaulted

down the steps and into the congregation, weaved through several groups of people who were shaking hands and hugging, and finally overtook Todd. Ben clapped him on the back and said, "Todd, my man!"

"Hey, Ben," answered the other.

Ben draped his arm over Todd's shoulder and squeezed his shoulders.

"Listen, I need a favor." He paused for a few seconds. "I really want to spend some time with Randi this afternoon, but if I go home with Dad, you know, for lunch, well . . ."

Ben stopped. Todd looked at Ben expectantly, until finally his eyes widened with realization.

"Oh," he said. "You want to come over to my house for lunch. Yeah, well sure. I'll check with Mom."

When Todd returned with the go-ahead, Ben secured his father's approval. Stifling a cry of victory that would have shocked the crowded church, Ben set out to find Randi.

He finally spotted her with her father at the front of the sanctuary, talking. Ben strolled toward them slowly. He approached just as the conversation ended and Pastor White slapped Ben's shoulder and spoke a few enthusiastic words of greeting to him.

Ben waited for Pastor White to get out of earshot. He then turned happily to Randi.

"Randi, listen. If all goes well, I'll be able to come over this afternoon and we can spend some time together." He went on to explain the arrangement with Todd, until Randi's expression choked off his words.

"What?" asked Ben. "What's wrong?"

"I'm sorry, Ben," she said. "Daddy needs me to play my guitar at the prison service this afternoon."

"I can't believe it," Ben said, moaning and throwing up his hands. "I mean, it's bad enough we live so far from each other, but you'd think since we both go to the same church that we'd see each other once in a while! *You're* here all the time, *I'm* here all the time, but I've seen people who *hate* each other spend more time together than we do."

"I know, Ben. I feel the same way you do. You know I do. We just have to be patient. Maybe Daddy'll give me the car for a little while on Saturday. I'll talk to him. Or maybe, when you get your driver's license—"

"I've got an idea," Ben interrupted her.

He searched frantically to come up with something to say. The words had just popped out of his mouth when Randi mentioned the license. Ben would change the subject whenever Randi talked about him driving. He had his learner's permit. But to get a license, he would have to pass a driver's education course. Driver's ed. was offered at school, of course. But then, Ben didn't go to school.

"Um, what if," Ben improvised, "what if Todd and I went to the prison meeting, too? Think your dad would mind?"

When Randi asked, Pastor White said he was pleased at the interest of Todd and Ben (Todd wasn't too pleased, but Ben had begged him).

Their small group inhaled lunch and proceeded to the prison. By the time they had cleared prison security and waited for the inmates to assemble in the auditorium, Ben feared that the afternoon was fading and, with it, whatever thin hope he had of spending time with Randi. The service crept along as Ben fidgeted and the inmates ogled Randi. Midway through the service, Ben noticed Pastor White speak into Randi's ear during the congregational singing.

While her father was reading the scripture, Randi edged to the chair beside Ben.

"Daddy wants to know if we'll sing a duet."

"A what?"

"A duet."

"What, you and me?"

"Yeah, something simple. He thinks the men would appreciate it."

"Like what?"

"Oh, I don't know." She paused. "Maybe something like 'Amazing Grace.' We can't go wrong with that."

Ben looked helplessly into Randi's delicate features. He couldn't say 'no' to her. " 'Amazing Grace,' huh?"

"Okay? You sing melody and I'll harmonize with you."

Moments later, Ben held a hymnal for Randi as they began to sing. Ben's mind galloped out of control. He felt the eyes of the convicts on Randi and struggled to concentrate on the song. He closed his eyes after the first line and continued singing, nervously, reading a line quickly, then closing his eyes to sing and opening them again to read the next line. Ben battled through three faltering verses of the hymn. After what seemed a lifetime of agony, the duet was over. The inmates, not allowed to rise to their feet, applauded vigorously, stomping their feet like a crowd at a football stadium.

Ben and Randi returned, red-faced, to their seats as

Pastor White delivered a meditation. A closing hymn and prayer followed.

"Finally," Ben whispered to Todd at the conclusion of the service. The prisoners lined the chapel wall in a sort of receiving line. Pastor White, Randi, Ben and Todd shook every hand as the inmates filed toward the auditorium exit. Near the end of the line, Ben spied a piece of paper pass from one inmate to Randi as she shook his hand.

"What was that?" Ben murmured in Randi's ear when they were safely outside the prison.

"Wait till we're in the van," she told him. They climbed into the van and Randi's father conspicuously adjusted the rearview mirror so that it framed not only the road, but his daughter and her boyfriend as well. Randi opened the piece of paper as Ben and Todd peeked over her shoulders.

The three of them deciphered the scrawled note:

> *My name is John Murphy.*
> *I get out in three weeks and I'd like to see you.*
> *Will you write to me?*
>
> *John Murphy 2947999*
> *Keller Correctional Facility*
> *2910 Tower Avenue*
> *Clearview, PA 17010*

Nobody said anything for a few moments. Finally, Ben broke the silence. "Well?"

"What do you mean, 'well?' " asked Randi.

"I mean, are you going to write him?"

"No, I'm not going to write to him."

"Good."

"I do kind of feel sorry for him though."

"You've got to be kidding," Ben exclaimed. "This guy's probably killed a few hundred people."

"Oh, Ben, don't be silly."

Ben felt his face turn red and realized that he was overreacting. But he couldn't cap the volcano of feelings that threatened to erupt inside him.

"All I know," he said, "is that you seem pretty pleased about that note."

Randi sighed.

"Ben, it's nothing, really," she said.

"You gonna save it?"

She threw him a disgusted look, lifted the note to his eyes, tore it in two and slid the pieces out the van window.

The quartet in the van lapsed into a painful silence. Randi stared out the window. Todd fought the urge to whistle as if nothing had happened and Pastor White drove on, apparently oblivious to all but the road.

They returned to the church as others were arriving for youth meeting. Ben looked at his watch.

This is ridiculous, he said to himself. *I left home at nine o'clock this morning and I'll get home at eight or nine o'clock tonight and in all that time I haven't spent more than two minutes alone with Randi.*

Pastor White parked the van.

Ben and Randi tumbled out together, as Todd awkwardly scuffed the bottom of his right foot across the pavement. Ben felt himself blushing. He grabbed

Randi's hand and squeezed.

"Randi, I'm sorry. I just . . ."

They stepped close together, facing each other. Behind them the van door slammed.

"Let's go," said Pastor White. "Time for youth meeting."

Randi smiled at Ben as they separated and walked with Todd into the church. Randi went to the front of the room to play her guitar for the choruses.

"You two sure know how to show a guy a fun time," Todd whispered to Ben as they were seated.

"I know, Todd, I'm sorry. Listen, nothing is working out right today. All I wanted was to spend some time with Randi and . . . and it turns out that some ax murderer made better time than I did."

Sometimes, thought Ben, *I think non-Christian kids must have it made. I mean, they don't have Sunday school to teach or youth meeting or any of that stuff. If Randi and I didn't spend so much time here . . . of course, if it weren't for church, I guess I'd never have met Randi. And the girls at school are all, well, I don't know, they're just not like Randi. Of course they're not, you jerk, 'cause Randi's a Christian.*

The youth meeting passed rapidly as Ben lost himself in thought.

And, after all, he told himself, *I'm happiest when I'm at church. Even before Randi, that's how it was. This is where my friends are.*

He surveyed the circle of teenage faces around the room.

My only friend at school, really, he reasoned, *is Charlie. I guess I'd have more friends if I went to classes. It's like*

I'm trapped, though. I just can't seem to make myself go to school. If only I could be the kind of person at school that I am here, you know? Confident, outgoing, happy—the ideal Christian teenager. That's a laugh. At school they all think I'm a junkie because I skip all the time. They'd croak if they knew the truth.

He pondered a moment longer.

Everybody here would croak, too, if THEY knew the truth.

After the meeting Ben turned to Todd. "I'm going to call my dad to come pick me up. How are you getting home? You need a ride?"

"Uh, yeah," Todd answered. "Yeah, I guess I do."

Ben and Todd stood around talking for a few minutes longer, but Ben soon ducked out of the room to make his call. The church office was dark when he arrived there, so he turned to go looking for someone to let him in to use the phone and nearly cracked heads with Randi.

"Daddy says we can use the van," she announced excitedly, "to take a bunch out to Mama's Pizza. C'mon, everybody's waiting for you."

Eight of the teens from youth meeting piled into the van—Ben and Todd, the twins Janice and Janey Tantino, "Hoop" Nelson, David and Kelly Watson and, of course, Randi, who drove.

This is it. This is the best time I've had all day, Ben told himself as he sat in the restaurant booth with his arm around Randi. The Tantino twins, in the next booth, were embarrassingly loud as usual, but other than that, the night was perfect.

They finished and left the restaurant after an hour

and a half. Randi dropped off David and Kelly at their house. Ben's trailer court was the next stop on the way. Randi passed Ben's trailer, continuing to the dead end, and turned around in the driveway of Lot #76. She then pulled the van even with Ben's trailer on the other side of the lane.

Ben jumped out and met Randi just as she was stepping out the driver's side. She closed her door gently and turned to face him. He started to put his arms around her, but stopped short. She was still facing him, but her eyes were fastened on the van window. The Tantino twins pressed their noses against the pane and grinned childishly at them.

"Walk me to the porch," Ben whispered. They strolled to the wooden porch of Ben's trailer and he began to embrace her again. He lowered his face slowly, and they kissed.

"What's wrong?" Ben asked as Randi drew back from him, shortening the kiss.

"Your father might be watching," she explained.

"He's not watching."

"*MY* father would be," she answered.

"I *know that*, but my dad's not overprotective like your dad. Besides, you think my dad thinks we don't kiss?"

"No, I just . . . It just makes me nervous."

"Just one more, then, a good one," he said and he kissed her goodnight.

She turned and walked back to the van. He stood on the porch, watching, until the van's taillights disappeared down the lane.

When Ben stepped inside, his father looked up from

the television.

"How'd it go at church all day?" he asked, returning his gaze to the set as he finished the question.

Ben crossed in front of him on his way to his bedroom.

"Great, Dad," he said. "It went great."

Chapter 3

Ben awakened Monday morning to a stupid jingle advertising acne medication on the clock radio. He slammed his hand down on the alarm button and groaned into the pillow.

With the jingle still playing in his mind, he trudged to the bathroom, flipped the light on and squinted into the mirror.

"Yeah, well, if it gets rid of unsightly blemishes," he growled, "what do you call these?"

His face was dotted with acne, some purple and swollen like an insect sting. He did the best he could with his face, then combed his hair to cover as much of it as he could.

He shuffled groggily to the kitchen and poured a glass of orange juice before returning to his bedroom. He sat on his bed. The sheets were tangled and knotted and the bare mattress peeked from where the bottom sheet had been wrenched free of the corner. As he sipped the juice, he remembered his resolution to go to school today.

"I'll get dressed, *then* I'll decide," he said, putting the juice glass down on his desk.

He poked the stereo button with his index finger and immediately began singing along with the song pulsing from the speakers.

He finished dressing, grabbed the juice and resumed his position on the unmade bed. He leaned forward, resting his elbows on his knees and holding the glass in both hands. He dozed in that position until his father thrust his head into Ben's bedroom door.

"You coming?" he asked. "You're going to be late." Ben jumped to his feet and followed his father into the living room. His dad stopped at the door.

"You going to leave the radio on all day?" Ben froze, then realized the music was still playing. "Oh," he said. He returned to his room and turned the stereo off, then closed his bedroom door behind him. *Keeping this door closed all the time*, he reminded himself, *sure did come in handy last Friday.*

Ben slumped in the front seat as his father drove the two miles to school. This time, though, instead of inching the car away before Ben had even closed the door, he put the car in "Park" and pulled something out of the sun visor.

Ben, suddenly worried, opened the door again, "What are you doing, Dad?"

He looked at Ben just as he licked a postage stamp. "I thought I'd drop these letters in that mailbox on the corner," he said.

Ben straightened and peered over the car roof toward the blue postal box at the end of the school driveway.

"Oh," he said, and closed the door again. He backed from the car a step or two. He couldn't very well stand there and wait for his father to pull away. After a moment of indecision, he turned and entered the building.

It felt strange being in the halls again. He looked at the milling students. *It's like the few seconds after you wake from a dream*, he reflected, *and you can't quite place the face of the person who woke you.* Ben had, of course, been in these halls many times before, but he'd been gone so long that they seemed oddly unfamiliar.

Just then Ben spied Mr. Billups, the biology teacher, striding toward him. He spun and shuffled toward the opposite end of the hall, hoping that Billups wouldn't spot him. He reached the glass door at the end of the hall and, without looking back, pushed the bar and stepped outside.

Once outside, Ben dashed to the low fence that separated school property from the back yards of a row of houses. Feeling like a CIA agent escaping a murderous enemy, he surveyed the yards quickly as he ran and aimed for one that seemed least likely to have any dogs or humans at home.

He vaulted the fence, raced through the yard to the street and only slowed after he'd counted five houses from the one where he'd jumped the fence.

Though Ben didn't know what street he was on, he managed to find his way to Benson Avenue and from there to Reading Road. He began to follow his customary route along the railroad tracks but stopped short when he remembered Friday's close call.

"I'm not going to let that happen again," he said.

Ben veered from the tracks back to Reading Road. There was a pancake house not far from the trailer court where his father often stopped for breakfast. Sometimes his father would leave from there for a day of making sales calls, but he would also occasionally return to the trailer after breakfast.

Ben approached the restaurant carefully, fearful that any minute his father would drive past, screech to a halt and ask, "Why aren't you in school, young man?"

He crossed the street to the sidewalk opposite the restaurant. He calculated that by stooping behind the cars that lined that side of the street, he could creep within sight of the parking lot without risk of being seen.

It worked as he had planned. He squinted through the windows of a dirty foreign car and spied his father's light brown Dodge in front of the sign with the giant stack of pancakes painted on it. The plastic letters on the sign read:

TO AY'S SPECIAL
BLUBBER Y PANCA ES SAUSAGE COFFEE

Ben smiled at the misspelling. *I bet they are blubbery pancakes*, he thought.

He was so distracted by the "blubbery pancakes," he didn't hear the man come up behind him.

"Hey, kid!" the man barked, and Ben jumped like he'd been kicked in the seat of the pants.

"Get off the car," the stranger said gruffly. Ben looked at him. He was a short, rumpled man who looked as unwashed as his car.

"Look a' that," he went on. "You've streaked the door all up!"

Ben glanced at the side of the car where he'd been leaning. The color of the car showed through the dirt where his jacket sleeve had wiped it clean.

You ought to get it washed, mister, Ben thought. *It wouldn't be streaked if it wasn't so dirty.*

The rumpled man flashed Ben one last irritated look as he climbed behind the steering wheel. With a grinding of gears, he pulled out and left Ben standing on the sidewalk where the car had been.

The incident with the man had so absorbed Ben's attention that it took a moment for him to realize that the barrier he'd hidden behind had deserted him and he was now in plain view of the pancake house. In the same instant, he saw his father exit the restaurant.

Ben ducked frantically behind the next car and crouched breathlessly in its shadow. Fighting to quiet the pounding of his heart, he knelt on the sidewalk and straightened to peek through the window of this car. He hesitated for a moment, looking up the walk in both directions to be sure he wouldn't encounter another irate car owner. Then he turned his gaze toward the pancake house, half expecting to see his father strolling in his direction to investigate.

Instead, he saw his father's car back out of the lot and pick up speed as it rolled down the street toward the trailer court.

Ben stood once more when his father's car was out of sight.

"Okay," he reasoned out loud, "What now,

Einstein?" He paced for a few minutes before making up his mind. Then he dodged the Reading Road traffic and cut between the buildings that separated the road from the train tracks.

As he balanced on the rails, the gears of his mind worked steadily. For some reason, Ben found that walking the tracks prompted some of his deepest thinking.

He began praying.

"Lord," he said as he walked, "I suppose I really should thank You for saving my hide back there."

He slipped off the rail briefly.

"I don't know why You did it, but I want You to know I really appreciate it."

That's stupid, he thought. *You know the Lord isn't the one who kept Dad from seeing you.*

Ben slowed his pace as he began speaking out loud.

"Listen, Lord, I know You can't be crazy about me skipping school and all that. I guess it is kind of like lying to Dad. And there's *no way* I could ever tell Randi the truth."

He neared the "overlook" point where he could see the trailer from the tracks.

"I know I shouldn't be doing this, Lord, but I've tried. You know I've tried. I've gone to school for almost a week at a time sometimes. But I can't . . . I don't know. *You* probably know more about my problem than *I* do. I just . . . I just can't get motivated, You know? School's got nothing for me. I just wish I could be the same way at school as I am at church."

He had arrived at the place. He squatted again to glimpse the trailer through the trees.

At least it's not muddy like it was Friday. He could see the trailer. *No dumb delivery truck, either.* But his dad's car stood in the driveway.

"Rats!" Ben drew his comb from his hip pocket and ran it carefully through his hair. It was a habit Ben performed so frequently that he no longer realized he did it. He replaced the comb.

He blew a long sigh between his lips. "Okay," he said, speaking as if there were another person present. "Here's what we'll do." He picked up a couple of pebbles and rattled them in his hand.

"We'll give him another half hour or so. Maybe he's just making a few calls like the other day. But if he doesn't leave by then . . ." Ben tossed the pebbles back into the dirt. ". . . if he doesn't leave then, well, then we'll have to find something to do for the rest of the day."

He rose and glanced up and down the tracks. "Yeah," he said. "Have to find something to do for the rest of the day."

Chapter 4

*B*en groaned as he sat on the cold steel rail. His head wavered listlessly on his folded arms which he propped on his bent knees. He raised his head to study his watch.

"It's now or never," he said as he stood erect. He limped on tingling, half-asleep legs to the trampled spot in the undergrowth where he stooped and peered through the foliage.

He let his chin drop to his chest and emitted a long sigh.

"Rats," he hissed. He lifted his head and took another look, as if to give the car in the driveway one last chance to redeem itself by disappearing. Then he turned and walked in the direction from which he'd come over thirty minutes earlier. After a dozen steps, he stopped, grappled in his hip pocket for his comb and withdrew it once more to slide it through his hair.

As he resumed his walk, he considered his options for the rest of the day.

I should have gone to school like I planned in the first

place. Of course, it's too late for that now.

His legs were fully awake now, so he hopped on the rail, balancing quickly from foot to foot. Something vibrated. Ben seemed to sense it, perhaps from the tracks. He strained, poised on one foot. The clacking cadence of an oncoming train sounded in the distance. He whirled. *Nothing in sight. Not yet.* His mind relaxed.

He turned to the day that yawned ahead of him. "I guess I could go to Spring Park," he reasoned aloud, "but that won't do for the whole day. The mall would be okay, except I don't have the bus fare." He spun and walked backward for a few steps. The train was visible now, though still a blurry speck in the distance. As he turned again to face the direction he walked, he hit on a solution.

"The bus station. Yeah, in fact, I won't even need money to get there."

Ben picked a spot in the bushes flanking the tracks and hopped down the slope to conceal himself from the approaching train. He waited there until the grimy, rusty cars reached him. Then he leaped from the bushes and trotted up the incline, matching his speed to that of the train as he jogged on the uneven rocks of the rail bed. He glanced ahead, then behind him as he ran to make sure no one saw him. Then carefully, his heart pumping in rhythm with the piston movement of his legs and the thump-clack sound of the train, Ben gripped the stepladder railing of the car beside him and swung, kicking and twisting and grasping, onto the bottom step.

"Oh, man, oh, man," he panted, clutching at his

heaving chest. He closed his eyes for a moment and fought to catch his breath as his fingers clenched the ladder. Finally, his breathing slowed. He looked around him from his perch on the lumbering train.

Panic gripped him suddenly as he realized that the train would soon be crossing Reading Road with him dangling from the ladder like furry dice in the windshield of a vintage car. His eyes darted over the cars lined at the railroad crossing, scanning them for his father's Dodge. He didn't see it. *Still,* he thought, *I can't let them see me. With my luck, a policeman would spot me and stop the train and . . .*

He gritted his teeth as he maneuvered his way from the ladder around the corner of the jostling car. The ground clacked by beneath him as he grabbed the bars on the rear of the freight car, his feet flaying the air wildly until they found the ledge beside the coupling. He clung desperately in that position, hugging the grimy metal as the train crossed the road.

Breathing easier, he shifted once more to find a more comfortable position and rode the three or four miles to his destination. As the train approached James Avenue, Ben stretched again to the ladder on the side of the car. Picking a fairly wide expanse of grass for a landing area, he sucked in a deep breath and jumped from the train.

His feet crashed the ground first, followed by his chin and nose. He pulled himself onto all fours and then lifted a finger to his nose, stifling an urge to sneeze. He wiped his face with his hand. No blood. Inhaling, he leaped to his feet, looked to his right and left, then began swaggering toward James Avenue.

Brushing his jacket and jeans, he relaxed into even strides.

Ben swung his arms freely as he walked down James Avenue in the direction of the bus station. The foul fumes of the bus engines assaulted him as he waited on the corner opposite the station for the walk light. Ben entered the doors of the station as the old fashioned electric clock below the schedules showed 9:55.

Feeling conspicuous, like a boy playing hookey, Ben strolled to the waiting area. He picked his way among the molded plastic chairs which held small coin-operated television sets.

I'll probably be lucky to find one that works, he figured, *let alone one that somebody left on.*

Most of the seats were empty, but in his search, Ben did have to sidestep a bag lady. His eyes darted over the heavily clothed woman, slumped in a chair. He didn't know if she was asleep. He didn't look at her face, only at her shopping bags, her blackened finger-nails and rumpled form.

Just past the lady, Ben paused to further survey the screens and spied a guy—*could be a college student*, he thought—hoist a duffel bag over his shoulder and desert his seat. Ben hustled to the vacant chair and slid in.

"All right," he said out loud as he discovered the lit screen. *Now, let's see what we can get.*

He flipped the channel selector from the game show that was playing. *Nothing*, he said to himself as each turn of the knob revealed interference. *Nothing*, he complained, as the channel selector returned to its original position, playing a snowy screen version of *Love Connection.*

"Great," he muttered as he slipped down in the chair, planted his chin in his hand and stared at the screen.

Seven minutes later the screen blackened. He glared at the blank box for a moment, then leaned his head to one side to read the label on the side.

"Fifty cents for fifteen minutes," he said. Even as he reached into his pocket to see what change he had, he said, "You're crazy. Fifty cents for fifteen minutes of *Love Connection,* no way."

He opened his palm.

Let's see, 80¢, 90¢, $1.27, no—$1.28. Better hold on to that in case I want a soda or something.

He shoved the money back into his pocket and lifted his head to look around. Snack bar, few people dozing in chairs, lady squinting through her glasses to read the bus schedule overhead, kid in a windbreaker, old janitor shuffling to a door to rattle his keys in the lock.

Pretty crummy place, he concluded. *I can't stay here all day. I'll go nuts.*

Ben tapped his fingers on the side of the television for a few moments before he let out a sigh and unfolded himself from the seat.

As he went out the same door he'd come through less than a half hour before, the guy in the windbreaker caught up to him.

"Hey, slick," he said to Ben once through the door, "What's up?"

Ben looked the kid in the face. *He's fifteen, maybe*

sixteen, he thought. He answered with an uncertain, "How's it goin'?"

" 'S alright," the kid said. "I got some action if you want it. Nickels, vials, what do you need?"

He stopped and waited, and Ben, feeling like he'd entered a room in the middle of a conversation, could only respond, "Huh?"

The kid rolled his eyes, looked away from Ben and had just begun to say something, but he halted before the first syllable was out. He hissed an obscenity as he stuffed both his hands and whatever they held into his jacket pockets. Without another word to Ben, the kid spun and began walking rapidly away.

Ben started to call after him, but as he did a realization suddenly swept over him. Immediately he knew what had just happened—what the kid was trying to say, and . . .

He jerked his head around to where the kid had been looking when he stopped short and met the eye of a man in a suit who was jumping out of a blue sedan.

Oh no, Ben thought. *He saw the kid trying to sell me some drugs.* He looked around again. The man shut the car door and began stepping toward Ben. Ben started walking in the direction the kid had gone.

What am I going to do? He probably thinks I bought from him. No, but I didn't, and all I have to do is stop walking right now and let the cop catch up to me and let him search me and he'll see I didn't buy anything.

Ben peeked behind him again. The man was calmly gaining.

This is stupid, he reasoned. *I'm a Christian. I have*

nothing to worry about from a cop. Except, he realized, *what if he decides to take me in anyway just to check me out or something? And what if he wonders why I'm not in school? What if he*—Ben was almost running now—*what if he calls the school? Or Dad?*

Ben broke into a full run on the sidewalk, glancing in the store windows along James Avenue to see reflections of the policeman's tie flapping in his face as he ran to catch him. Ben's eyes widened in panic as he ran. His mind pounded, *oh man, oh man,* with his pumping legs.

I got him beat. I got him beat. He began to get excited with optimism as the cop seemed to lose ground behind him.

I got him beat.

Then he saw the blue sedan. It had pulled to the curb at the intersection a half block away. The door on the driver's side started to open.

I'm dead. Oh, man.

An alley opened abruptly on his right, and Ben ducked quickly into it without losing a step. Too late he saw the sign at the corner:

DEAD END

Hardly thinking, he stopped, twirled and ran full tilt back out the alley, ducking his head just in time to slip under the outstretched arm of his pursuer who was reaching for the corner of the building to steady himself.

Ben kicked his heels back in the direction from which he'd just come. A quick glance over his shoulder assured him that his maneuver in the alley turned out to his advantage. The two detectives now pursued him shoulder-to-shoulder instead of from two directions, and he seemed to have widened the gap more than before his reversal of direction.

His chest ached now; it felt the size of a beach ball.

I can't slow down now, he told himself. *If they catch me now, they'll figure I ran because I'm guilty. They'll never believe I'm just skipping school. They'll probably think I ditched the drugs in the alley.*

Feeling that any minute his chest would explode, Ben dodged the traffic and crossed the street into a parking lot. He stooped as he ran between the cars and vans. Emerging from the lot, he rounded a corner and headed for the trees and bushes that lined the area where the train tracks crossed James.

He stole a glance again over his shoulder as he ran.

No cops.

He neared the bushes and turned again to look.

No cops.

He turned his body sideways and slid into the bushes, dropping to the dirt and crawling on hands and knees for a few yards before stopping. Lying flat on his belly, he peered out from the cover of the bushes as he waited for the policemen to appear.

Maybe I lost them, he supposed, feeling like a TV detective who's just "shaken a tail."

He still found it difficult to breathe quietly and a sharp pain knifed up his side. The coolness of the ground began to penetrate his clothes and as the minutes ticked by, he began to feel cramped and itchy but was afraid if he moved he might be noticed.

Or worse, he imagined, *I might attract the attention of a passing dog.*

Finally convinced that the two men from the blue sedan had given up the chase, Ben crawled from the bushes and walked briskly between the tracks toward home.

"That was too close," he said, still glancing furtively around for a sign of the policemen. He looked at his watch.

"Man," he said. "I still have half the day to kill." He strode from tie to tie to tie. Soon, though, he tired of that irregular rhythm and stepped onto the silver rail, balancing as he walked, holding his arms slightly away from his body. After a minute or two of that he slid off the rail and walked between the tracks again.

"This is crazy," he said. "I've got to be out of my mind."

He calculated that the walk back to Reading Road would take, maybe, an hour. Then he'd have to find something to do until it was safe to show up at the trailer.

"I am *definitely* going back to school tomorrow," he said.

Chapter 5

"Hey, AWOL! Hey, AWOL! Wait up!" Charlie Parker flagged Ben across the corner parking lot of the A & P. Ben halted and waited, smiling at his friend.

"Skip school again?" Charlie asked when he reached the waiting truant.

Ben nodded his head with a half smile.

Charlie fell in step with Ben in the direction of the trailer park. "What did you do all day?"

Ben told him all that had happened, how he'd hopped the train to James Avenue, watched television at the bus station, been approached by the kid selling drugs and ran from the cops.

"Get outta here," Charlie said, unbelieving.

"No, I'm serious," Ben responded and went on to tell how, after he escaped the men in the blue sedan, he spent the rest of the afternoon at Spring Park, watching the ducks, old people and small children until school let out, and he figured it was safe to start for home.

When Ben had finished his recitation, Charlie

slapped him on the back.

"Well *I* have something to tell *you*," he said. Ben couldn't keep from smiling at the stupid grin pasted on Charlie's face as he proposed to let Ben in on his bit of knowledge.

"Yeah?"

"Yeah," Charlie said. "Billups stopped me in the hall today."

Ben's smile disappeared. He waited for Charlie to continue.

"He was asking about you."

"Yeah, what'd he say?"

"Well, first he asked me, 'Say, Parker,' " Charlie said, mimicking the biology teacher's nasal voice. " 'Aren't you a friend of Ben Howard?' "

He must've seen me skip out this morning, Ben thought.

"So I said, 'Sure,' and he said, 'How come the school office can never get hold of his father? He does live with his father,' he said, 'doesn't he?' And I said, 'Yeah,' I said, 'but his dad's a salesman or something and he doesn't usually get home until five or six o'clock at night.' " Charlie paused and looked at Ben as they both stopped walking. "What?" he asked, in response to Ben's stare.

"You told him that?" Ben answered.

"Yeah, why? What?"

"Charlie, you know what he's gonna do?" Ben held his hands out, palms up, in a gesture of helplessness. "He's going to call Dad, that's what. At night. When he's home."

The look on Charlie's face showed that he missed the full significance of that.

"You mean the school's never tried to call your dad about your absences before?"

"No," Ben said. "Well, yeah, they have, but always during school hours when I'm home to tell them I'm sick or to imitate Dad and say, 'Yes, thank you, young Ben is home with my permission'."

Charlie stared blankly at Ben for a moment. Then he simply said, "Oh."

Ben whipped his comb out and pulled it through his hair.

"So," he said, "now I have to figure out a way to keep Billups from connecting with Dad."

They entered the trailer park in silence. Charlie was feeling bad for having messed things up for Ben. Ben tried desperately to finagle a way out of this fix.

Charlie smiled apologetically at Ben as he ascended the steps to his trailer, Lot #60. "See ya later," he said to Ben. Ben waved to him absentmindedly, like he was batting at a fly.

He was still wrestling with his problem as he climbed the porch steps to his own trailer. As he opened the door, the phone rang. Ben dove across the room with a violent effort, calling loudly as he did, "I got it!"

He snatched the receiver, bobbled it briefly and finally clamped it to the side of his face, bellowing a fatherly "Hello" as he did. There was a moment of silence on the other end of the line before a girl's voice spoke timidly.

"Ben? Ben, is that you?"

Ben relaxed.

"Oh, hi, Randi." He cleared his throat. "Yeah, it's me."

"Oh," she said in a confused tone. "It didn't sound like you."

Ben's dad walked out of his bedroom at the opposite end of the trailer. Ben cupped his hand over the mouthpiece.

"It's Randi," he whispered. Then, into the phone, he said, "I'm sorry. I just walked in the door." With a glance in his dad's direction he added, "Just got home from school this minute."

Ben eyed his father suspiciously as he and Randi talked over the day's events.

Billups could've called Dad before I got home. He did seem a little funny when he came into the room. Maybe he's waiting until I get off the phone and then he'll say something like, "Ben, I got a call today from your school."

"The main thing I wanted to tell you," Randi was saying, "is that I've got some unbelievable news for you." Ben steered his attention back to the conversation with Randi, like jarring a phonograph needle that's been stuck in a groove.

"What news?"

"Oh, it's good news. Unbelievable news! It's sort of about us. But I don't want to tell you over the phone. Can we go out for a little while tonight? What if I come over and pick you up?"

"That'd be great," he started to say, but then he remembered. *Mr. Billups. He's supposed to call here tonight. I can't go out. What if he calls while I'm gone?* "Uh, except I can't," he told her. *What do I tell her?*

"You can't?" Randi didn't sound upset, only pleading.

"No, I'm really sorry, Randi, but I . . ." *What to say?*

"Well, it's a long story. Why? What's so big about your news that you can't tell me over the phone?"

"I guess it'll just have to wait, now, won't it?" she teased.

"How about tomorrow?"

"Okay. I'll see if Daddy will let me use the van tomorrow night. I suppose I can keep the surprise that long. But it won't be easy."

Ben hung up a moment later, a little angry that he had to pass up an opportunity to spend time alone with Randi. Shielding the phone from his father's view, he gingerly pinched the cord at the back of the phone to disconnect it. *Now,* he said to himself, *if I can just keep Dad from using the phone for the rest of the night, I should be set.* He turned to face his dad, who had been sitting on the couch during Ben's phone conversation, the contents of several file folders spread in front of him on the coffee table.

"So, Dad," Ben began, thinking *Let's get it over with now; if you've already talked to Mr. Billups, you might as well give me the sentence now and save me a lot of worry and trouble.* "What are we going to do for dinner?"

Mr. Howard slowly removed his glasses from his nose and set them on the papers.

Here it comes, Ben thought. He visualized scenes of horror, blue-suited men escorting him roughly to a scummy prison cell, his screams of horror echoing down the lonely corridors.

His father said, "Any suggestions?"

Ben momentarily forgot his question. *Oh, yeah,* he recalled with relief, *about dinner.*

"Uh, well, no," he stammered. *Looks like Billups*

hasn't called yet.

Since Ben's mom had died, he and his dad usually ate out because neither of them had any gift for cooking. But after months on end of restaurant food, Ben had habitually complained over his father's choice of eateries and lamented his unfamiliarity with home-cooked meals. But tonight, the last thing Ben wanted was a quiet meal at home. He had to get his father out of the house.

"I was thinking," he said, culling his mind for the slowest, most distant restaurant he could remember. "How about Old Farm?"

His father raised his eyebrows in an expression of surprise.

"Way out there?"

Ben started to work up an explanation, but his father paused only briefly before continuing.

"Any other night, Ben, that'd be a welcome suggestion, but tonight I'm afraid I have too much work to do. Suppose we just order out for pizza?"

Ben started to protest and argue with his father, but Mr. Howard stood from the couch and said, "What's the number for the pizza place?"

Ben turned frantically to the disconnected phone and said, over his shoulder and a little too loudly, "I'll call, Dad. What do you want on it?" As his father listed pizza toppings, Ben plugged the phone cable in, thinking, *I'm dead. Of all the nights he has to stay in and order pizza. It's got to be tonight. I'm cursed. If Billups calls, my life is over.*

He punched the numbers of the pizza shop. *I can't even tie up the phone with Randi, now that she thinks I've got something keeping me busy all night.*

"Hello. Yes, I'd like a large pizza with pepperoni, sausage, green peppers and mushrooms, for delivery."

"And onions," his father added without looking up from his work.

"And onions," Ben echoed. *If I leave the phone disconnected all night and he finds it, he's gonna know something's up.*

"Yeah," Ben spoke again. "At 9797 Reading Road." He paused. "Lot #67."

Guess I could call Charlie. Though talking to him all night is going to be a real test of my will. Charlie's a super friend, but he's not a brilliant conversationalist.

"Okay, thanks." He concluded his exchange with the pizza shop and flopped the phone back in the cradle. He kept his hand on the receiver as he considered his next course of action.

Then the phone rang.

Terror seized Ben's heart like a hawk snatches a rabbit. His dad sat just feet away. *What will I say if it's Billups?*

On the second ring, his dad looked up from his work. Ben smiled weakly at him and lifted the phone to his ear.

"Hello?" His voice was a dry rasp.

"Hey, AWOL, how's it goin'?" It was Charlie.

"Charlie! Man, am I glad you called."

"Has Billups called yet?"

Ben thought *I'm still alive, aren't I?*

"No," he said. Then softly, hoping his father wasn't listening, he added, "Charlie, can you come over? I need your help with something and I can't really discuss it over the phone." He winced as he said that, remembering that Randi was holding some big news for him. But that would have to wait.

"Now? I gotta leave in a half hour to go to the mall with my uncle."

Rats! Ben couldn't believe how things were working against him today. *Charlie can't very well help me from Bainbridge Mall.* Then an idea started to form in Ben's mind.

"Hold on for a second, Charlie." He cupped his hand over the mouthpiece and held the phone in his lap while he thought this one out. After a few moments, he spoke again into the phone.

"Just come over, Charlie. Now. It'll just take a minute."

Ben had a plan.

Chapter 6

$\mathcal{B}$en met Charlie on the trailer porch, quietly but firmly closing the door behind him. He thought about stepping around the trailer where he would be sure his father couldn't hear, but decided instead to remain close to the door so he could jump to the phone if Billups called.

"Okay, here's the deal," he said to Charlie. "You're going to the mall with your uncle."

It sounded like a statement, but Charlie discerned from Ben's face that he wanted an answer.

"Yeah, why?"

"I need a big favor from you, Charlie. I have to get Dad out of the house."

Charlie listened intently. Ben didn't have to explain why he had to lure his father out; Charlie understood. He even felt responsible, since he had been the one who told Billups about Mr. Howard being home nights.

"So I was thinking. You go to the mall with your uncle. After you're there for a few minutes, lose him. But not for long. When you come back a couple minutes later, explain to him that you've met a group of friends and they'll bring you home."

A look of doubt crept into Charlie's expression. Ben noticed and talked a little faster.

"Then when everything's set, you run to the nearest pay phone and call me. I'll explain to Dad that you're stranded out at the mall, that the friends you were with left you there or something—I don't know, just leave that end of it to me—and we'll come out, pick you up, bring you home, and I will owe you for the rest of my life."

Ben placed a hand on Charlie's shoulder to add to the persuasion of his words. Charlie's face bore an expression of distaste, as if he'd just sucked a sour lemon.

"I don't know, AWOL," he said slowly.

"Charlie," Ben pleaded. "I need this."

They stared at each other for a long time. Charlie was the first to look away.

"What if . . .," Charlie said as he looked at his feet, "what if my uncle doesn't go for it?"

Ben ducked his head as if to lift Charlie's chin with his gaze.

"Charlie," he said. Ben's technique apparently worked, because Charlie lifted his head and met Ben's eyes. "He *has* to go for it."

Charlie shrugged and said, "Okay," without conviction. Ben watched him plod back toward his trailer. Then, with a deep breath, he turned and went inside.

The pizza came soon after that. Ben sat in the chair by the phone, watching TV as he ate. His father worked steadily, occasionally taking a bite of pizza from the plate beside him on the couch.

As he gathered the remains of the pizza and the dishes, Ben realized he had no idea what show he'd just been watching. He'd been lost in thought about the corner he'd painted himself into. He couldn't go out with Randi because he had to prevent Mr. Billups from connecting with his dad. He couldn't call Randi either, which would accomplish the dual purpose of tying up the phone while talking to his girl. And now, his brilliant plan kept him from disconnecting the phone because he had to wait for Charlie's call from the mall.

So I just have to hang around here, he grieved, *and die a slow, agonizing death.*

For forty-five minutes after he cleared the dinner dishes, Ben awaited the call. He tried to watch TV. He flipped through a magazine. He even scanned next Sunday's lesson for his class, but he always stayed in the living room, always close to the phone.

Finally the phone rang.

Ben jerked to his feet and struggled to act nonchalant as he ambled the few steps to the phone.

"Hello? Charlie," he said. "It's about—uh, what's up?" He observed out of the corner of his eye that his father was still buried in his work.

"Uh huh . . . yeah, uh huh." Charlie was relating the difficulties he'd had arranging things like Ben had said and how much this favor was going to cost him. Ben, conscious of his father's ear just a few feet away, responded only with, "Uh huh" and "yeah."

Finally, he said, "Hold on Charlie, I'll ask," and smothered the phone in his hands.

"Dad?"

His father still bent over his work.

"Hey, Dad?"

He looked up at him over the tops of his glasses.

"Uh, Charlie's out at Bainbridge Mall and he's, uh, he's stranded. His, uh, the group of kids he was with left him there, and he wants to know if we can come out and give him a ride home."

Mr. Howard sat upright, closed his mouth and exhaled through his nose. He looked displeased.

"He said he's really sorry . . ."

Ben's father opened his mouth, closed it, then opened it again and said flatly, "I'll get my jacket."

Ben and his father rode in silence to the mall. Ben had arranged the meeting place with Charlie before hanging up, and Charlie was waiting. He didn't look at Ben as he climbed in, and after the initial exchange of a reluctant "thank-you" and an equally reluctant "you're welcome" between Charlie and Mr. Howard, the homeward ride also passed in silence.

As Ben and his father entered the trailer after letting Charlie out at his lot, Mr Howard walked back to his bedroom to hang up his jacket. Ben tiptoed to the phone and pinched the jack once more.

Just in case, he reasoned, *though Billups wouldn't call this late.*

He said good night to his dad, who had immediately returned to his work on the coffee table.

Ben stepped into his room. He shut the door behind him, turned on the radio and looked in the mirror over his desk.

"Made it," he said out loud to his unsmiling reflection.

Chapter 7

Ben didn't go to school on Tuesday. He had planned to when he went to bed Monday night, but at 6:00 a.m. his father knocked politely on the bedroom door and poked his head inside.

"Ben?"

He waited for some indication of life from the jumbled, sleeping tangle of arms, legs and sheets that was Ben.

"Ben?" he said, louder.

A hoarse groan erupted from the bed.

"Ben, I have to leave early this morning. If you get up now, you'll be able to walk to school in plenty of time." He waited for a signal of comprehension.

"Ben!" He didn't shout but his deep voice resounded.

The body on the bed moved.

"Yeah, okay. If I get up now, I can make it to school on time."

As his dad stood in the doorway, Ben hoisted himself into a sitting position on the edge of the bed and hung his head like a prisoner waiting death. Moments later, he stumbled groggily into the bathroom; his father collected his papers and file folders from the coffee table and crammed them into his briefcase as he trod to the bathroom door.

"Ben," he said through the closed door. "I'm leaving now. Have a good day, okay?"

Still struggling to work his jaw muscles this early in the morning, he responded, "Yeah, Dad. Thanks."

As he listened to his father's retreating steps, he realized that he should have wished him a good day, too. He returned to his room and peeked through the window over the bed. The car was gone. He cast a sleepy eye at the clock. 6:12. *It's too early to go to school*, he resolved. *I'm going back to sleep.*

Over four hours later, Ben dragged himself out of bed a second time that day. This time, however, he showered and dressed. He devoured two bowls of cold cereal while watching a late morning game show on TV.

The rest of the day he listened to music, alternating between FM radio and his extensive CD collection, read, and watched TV. When three o'clock rolled around, he walked to the phone. Biting a nail, he decided he'd better call Charlie.

He lifted the receiver, punched Charlie's number, and raised the phone to his ear. For a split second he was startled. Then, remembering the events of last night, he reached a hand behind the phone and connected the cable. He redialed the seven digits. Charlie answered on the third ring.

"Hi, Charlie. It's me, Ben."

"Yeah, hi, AWOL." Charlie's voice was expressionless.

"Listen, thanks for what you did last night. I know it was a real pain, but I couldn't have done it without you."

Silence.

Ben spoke again, "You're mad, aren't you?"

"No."

"Yes, you are, Charlie. I can tell."

"I'm not mad, okay?"

"Okay. Sorry. Did you see Billups today?"

"I don't know. Yeah, I guess. Passed him in the hall. I guess."

"Did he say anything?"

"No."

"You *are* mad."

"I am not. He didn't say anything."

"He didn't ask about me or say he tried to call my Dad?"

"No, I'm telling you he didn't say anything, all right?"

"Yeah, okay. I just want to be sure he's not going to try to call again. I couldn't take another night like last night."

"Yeah."

"Okay, Charlie. See ya later, okay?"

Charlie hung up without another word. *He's mad*, Ben thought. *I can tell.* He sat for a few moments.

"He'll get over it," he said finally, dismissing Charlie from his mind.

He glanced at his watch. *Randi should be home by now*, he figured. He picked up the phone again and pressed the pattern of her number without even thinking of the number itself.

Randi's younger sister Meghan answered the phone. Randi spoke from the extension as soon as Ben asked for her.

"Oh, Randi," Ben said. "You're there."

"Yeah. I picked up at the same time Meghan did."

The conversation stalled.

"You can hang up now, Meghan," Randi said.

"Okay. Bye, Ben." A loud click followed.

Silence again floated over the telephone.

"Hang up, Meghan," Randi repeated. Randi and Ben waited for the careful return of the phone to its cradle.

"Okay," Randi said into the receiver. "She's gone now."

They exchanged the usual accounts of the day's events; Ben said as little about school as he could, trying to give the impression of a normal day in the life of a high school junior.

"So, what's the big news you've got to tell me?"

"I'll tell you tonight," she replied. "Daddy said I could have the van for a couple of hours. What time should I come over?'

They agreed on the details of the evening and went on to talk about the jeans Randi found on sale at The Denim Place and the new song she heard on the radio this morning—"It made me think about us. It *was* about us"—and what Janice Tantino had said on the way home Sunday night after they'd dropped Ben off at the trailer.

Randi usually did most of the talking; this time she

did even more than usual because Ben had nothing new to report to her. He couldn't tell her about yesterday's events at the bus station, nor about his struggle to prevent Billups from contacting his Dad. He couldn't tell her the truth about how he spent today, either. He hated lying to Randi, though he did it often whenever she asked about classes or grades or teachers.

"Daddy says I have to go," Randi said finally. Ben swung his wrist in front of him and glanced at his watch. They'd been talking for well over an hour.

"See you soon," Randi promised. They exchanged a few awkward moments of affection and Ben dropped the phone into its place.

His ear tingled from the prolonged pressure of the earpiece as he sat motionless in the dim trailer.

What would she do if she knew, he asked himself. *Would she still date a guy who's flunked his freshman year—twice?*

The lengthening shadows of the dwindling day matched Ben's mood as he pondered his predicament.

It'd probably be just the kind of thing Jason Adams has been waiting for, Ben thought. Randi had never gone out with Jason, but it wasn't because Jason hadn't tried.

He couldn't believe it when Randi started going with me, Ben remembered. *Of course, I couldn't believe it, either. Jason always figured he was better looking and more talented than me, so why shouldn't she prefer him?*

He let out a lone chuckle.

"Yeah, well," he said aloud in the quiet room, "that's

the way I figured it, too."

He stood.

"Lucky for me, Randi didn't see it that way, or I'd have never had a chance."

Ben's father came in about forty-five minutes later, as Ben was carefully positioning his hair to cover as many blemishes as possible. He turned from his bedroom mirror as his father passed his door and shouted the news of his plans through the trailer's thin walls. He waited for a response. When a minute or two passed without a sound from his father's direction, Ben went to his father's room and peeked in.

His father's body lay sprawled on the bed, his legs bent over the side, as if he had sat down to remove his shoes and had collapsed onto the bed, asleep.

"Dad?"

A brief grunt issued from the form on the bed. Ben wasn't sure that his father was awake, but he repeated himself, saying that he and Randi were going to Mama's for a little while and he'd be back in time to do his homework and could he borrow, like, five dollars or maybe ten, if that was okay?

His father creaked to an upright position on the bed like a massive statue being hoisted by a crane. He fished out the money. Ben took it.

"Tough day?"

His father responded with another grunt and fell back onto the bed. Ben tiptoed out of the room and returned to the mirror in his bedroom for another hair check.

I probably should do something more for him, Ben thought. *He looks like he had an awful day. Maybe I should go back in and see if he wants to talk.* He shrugged at his reflection in the mirror. *Nah,* he thought. *Let him sleep. That's probably what he needs most.*

The beep of a horn outside signaled Randi's arrival. Ben hurried out and jumped into the passenger seat, thinking again how humiliating it was not to have a driver's license. Randi leaned his direction and they exchanged a brief kiss.

"So," Ben started, "what's the big news? You're killing me."

She flashed a knowing smile at him as she started driving. "You'll have to wait. At Mama's. When our pizza comes."

"Man, you're making this into a real Hollywood production, aren't you? Is it really that big?"

"It's really that big."

"You know what you're going to do, don't you? You're going to build me up and lead me on until, when you finally tell me, it's going to be a letdown. It'll never be as big as what you're building it up to be. So you might as well just tell me now."

He leaned back in the van seat and smiled proudly at his reasoning. Randi smiled back at him as if she were laughing inside.

"I'm not worried," she asserted as she steered the van expertly into Mama's parking lot.

Randi and Ben chatted comfortably and affectionately in Mama's darkened interior as they waited for their pizza. Ben tried several times to extract the "big news" from Randi, but his efforts were only half serious. He knew that she wanted to do this in her own way. She wanted everything to be perfect. She'd even insisted that they wait a few extra minutes until the waitress had finished clearing the table so they could sit in "their booth."

When the pizza arrived, Ben dished a piece for each of them and leaned across the table. Randi leaned in, too, until their faces were nearly touching. After a short prayer over the steaming pizza, Ben opened his eyes and smiled. He was enjoying this.

Finally Randi announced, "We're moving."

His expression stiffened immediately. "What?"

"We're moving," she repeated. Then, noticing the emotion in his face, she added, hurriedly, "Oh, not farther away. Closer."

Ben relaxed slightly.

"Where?" he asked.

Randi licked her lips. Restrained excitement showed in her face.

"Verona!" she shrieked.

"Verona?" Ben echoed.

"Yeah, can you believe it?" She drummed the table excitedly with her open palms. "Daddy told us Sunday night. I've been dying to tell you. Isn't it great?"

"Yeah," Ben said, his mind spinning with thoughts tumbling around, over and through one another. "Yeah, unbelievable."

"I mean, it's perfect, Ben. We'll not only live a lot closer to each other, but . . ." she leaned closer until their eyes were only inches apart, then she whispered, "we'll be going to school together."

Chapter 8

$\mathcal{B}$en struggled to control his panic. He felt like a rodeo cowboy wrestling a calf, only he was wrestling his mind. He felt as though Randi had set her hair on fire, and now she was sitting there staring at him, waiting for him to smile happily.

Did I hear correctly? Did she say, "We'll be going to school together"? I think she did. That must be what she said. She's smiling. I'm supposed to be happy.

He froze for what seemed an eternity. He strained to control his facial muscles, to keep the panic from showing in his expression.

I've got to say something.

Randi beamed from the other side of the table, patiently waiting for Ben to scream or throw his arms around her or whatever a normal high school student would do with this kind of news.

I've got to say something. Ben searched his mind for a response. *Something convincing.*

"Wow!" *Stupid.* He could have kicked himself as soon as he said it.

"I know. It's unbelievable, isn't it?" Randi said. "I felt the same way when Daddy told us the night before last. I think I screamed, but I was just like you are now!"

As she spoke, a flood of relief washed over Ben. She had interpreted his awkward reaction as surprise. *She's got that right,* he thought. And her rush of words gave Ben the moment that he needed to collect himself to answer more profoundly when she stopped.

"Yeah," he said.

"I still can't believe it," Randi gushed. "Who knows, maybe we'll get study hall together or something like that."

"Yeah," he mumbled through a mouthful of pizza. Randi bubbled excitedly about how she'd hardly slept at all Sunday night and how disappointed she was when Ben couldn't go out last night so she could tell him then and how she'd been tempted "a *million* times" to just call him and tell him over the phone but how she wanted this to be special since it was such "totally perfect" news and she was *so* glad she'd waited so she could tell him in person, right across the table from each other and . . .

"When?"

"Huh?"

Ben's interruption had been drowned out by her flurry of words so that she didn't hear him clearly.

"When?" he repeated. That vital question had suddenly occurred to him. *If she's not moving until the end of the school year, that gives me time to do something, to get myself back on track.*

"When are you moving?" he clarified his question.

"Oh," she said, and leaned closer to tell him. The waitress came at that moment and asked, "May I get you anything else?" When they answered negatively, she slid the check toward Ben's elbow and retreated into the dimness of the restaurant once more.

They faced each other again.

"The end of next week," she said, arching her eyebrows and smiling as if she had just delivered the punch line of a hilarious joke.

"The end of next week?" Ben's voice rose like a squeaky violin on the last word. "Wow," he said again, quietly.

Randi again agreed with the sentiment she thought Ben was expressing. She went on to talk excitedly of all the things they'd be able to do together, all the time they'd have to spend together. Ben's thoughts traveled a different track altogether.

The end of next week. That tears it, he thought. *It's over. She's going to know all about me, now. My skipping school, my lying to Dad. My lying to her, to everybody at church. Man, my whole life's been a lie. Well, almost. I mean, the way I feel about Randi, that's not a lie. And the way I am at church, too, that's real. I guess it's just school. I can't be the kind of person at school that I am at church. But, heck, anybody can be a Christian at church.*

Ben did his best to look involved in Randi's conversation while panic pulsed in his head. He glanced around the restaurant. All the booths he could see were empty. He stole a look at his watch. It was getting late.

He gazed at Randi's face with new appreciation. *She's so pretty,* he thought. *Look at her. Man, I'm so lucky.*

Or was.

Randi had stopped talking and the two of them sat wordlessly holding hands across the table. Ben felt his eyes swelling with tears.

I might as well tell her now and get it over with. Ben inhaled deeply and pressed his palms to the table to brace himself.

"Randi . . ."

"Excuse me," interrupted the waitress, "do you want me to put the rest of that pizza in a box for you?" She looked impatient.

Ben and Randi looked at her, then at each other, then to the pizza. Most of it remained untouched on the tray.

"Uh, yeah, I guess so," said Ben. "Please," he added as an afterthought.

Randi stood.

"We'd better go, huh?" She rolled her eyes in the direction of the anxious waitress.

Ben paid for the pizza at the register, returned to the table to leave a tip and picked up the boxed pizza on his way out.

They exchanged only scattered words on the short drive to the trailer park.

Maybe I'll tell her when she stops the van in front of the trailer. I'll spin around in my seat to face her. I'll take both of her hands in mine, and I'll level with her.

He formulated what he would say.

Randi, I'm not the man you think I am.

Randi, I love you too much to go on lying to you.

Randi, what if I were only a freshman? Would you still go out with me?

Randi, I've been involved in a secret government project that has kept me out of school for the last two years. I wish I could tell you more, but it'll have to be our secret. . . .

"Here we are," Randi said. "I didn't expect to be out this late. Hope your dad's not mad."

"No," Ben shrugged. "He'll be okay." He spun in his seat and faced her. He reached for her hands and held her thin fingers lightly. His throat tightened and his eyes began to cloud.

"Randi," he said. She waited as if she knew something momentous was about to occur. "Tell your dad I'm sorry I kept you out so late."

They kissed, and Ben stepped down from the van. He mounted the trailer steps and turned as he grabbed the screen door handle. He waved as the van rolled out of sight.

Ben was relieved to discover that his father had already gone to bed. He poured a glass of orange juice and took it into his room. He switched the desk lamp on, poked the stereo to life, kicked one shoe off, then the other, and sat on his bed with his back against the wall, sipping the juice every couple minutes.

He slumped in that position without moving, except to lift the glass to his lips and occasionally mouth the words of a song. Every song reminded him of Randi. His eyes blurred with tears every few minutes and his nose frequently tingled as if he were about to sneeze.

He changed position only once, to reach to the top of his dresser for the framed photo of Randi. He laid it next to him on the bed and glanced at it now and then.

As the minutes flipped by on his clock radio, Ben sank steadily deeper into depression. Finally, as the digits on the clock flashed 2:17, he returned the photo to its place on the dresser, set the juice glass on the floor by the bed, stretched to turn off the desk lamp and undressed hurriedly in the dark, letting his clothes drop to the floor. He slid between the sheets and laid his head on the pillow. Every few minutes he discovered that he had to move the pillow. The wetness bothered him.

Chapter 9

$\mathcal{B}$en awoke with a start the next morning. *It was a dream*, he thought. Then he surveyed the room and saw the juice glass and the clothes he'd worn to Mama's. Reality crashed into him again like a slap in the face with a sopping dishrag.

"My life is over," he groaned. His head throbbed and his eyes still felt puffy from last night's tears. He cast a bleary eye toward the clock.

Time to get up. I'm surprised Dad hasn't come in yet. He must have had as bad a day yesterday as I did. He lay his head back on his pillow. *No*, he decided. *No living thing could ever have a day that bad . . . except me.*

Moments later, Ben's father came to the door and announced that they were a little late, so they'd better hurry.

"Dad, I can't go to school today. I'm sick." He was too tired and depressed to even manage the usual routine of deception that had been his habit for the past two years.

His father entered the room and sat on the side of

Ben's bed. Ben explained that he had a headache and felt "totally awful." *And that's no lie,* he told himself.

"And I haven't missed any school in a long time," he pleaded. *Okay,* he admitted to his conscience, *that was a lie. But it was necessary.* He pondered a moment. *Rats!* he thought. *I should have said, "I haven't stayed home sick for a long time." That would have been the truth.*

"Well," his father responded thoughtfully, "maybe you do need to stay home. I'll check and see if we have anything for you to take for your headache." He started toward the bathroom, but halted at the doorway. "Do I need to call the school to tell them you're sick?"

"No!" Ben responded too quickly, he realized. "Uh, no, Dad," he continued, forcing himself to appear calm. "No, you can just write me a note to take in tomorrow."

His father hesitated, then nodded and strode to the bathroom. Ben closed his eyes and escaped again into sleep. He didn't hear his father return with the small plastic bottle of aspirin. He also was oblivious to his father's later movements about the trailer as he dressed and fixed a cup of instant coffee and a bowl of cereal. He didn't stir when his father's car coughed to life outside the window over his bed.

He slept heavily, motionless, until after noon. When he finally managed to lift his weighty head from the pillow, he enjoyed one blissful moment before he remembered last night.

"My life is over," he said. He leaned over to turn up the volume of the stereo and sat groaning, reliving the conversation at Mama's that had signaled the end of his dream year with Randi.

As a reflex, he lifted his gaze to Randi's image on the dresser. He unconsciously placed his palm on his chest. It felt hollow, as if some invisible creature had crept in during the night and bit into it, leaving a large concave area, allotting him little space to breathe.

He stumbled to the bathroom in his underwear. He washed. He brushed his teeth. He combed his hair. He applied medication to his acne. He trudged to the kitchen. He gulped down a glass of orange juice in one swallow. He ate a bowl of cereal at the table while he sat, in his underwear, staring out the window at the side of the next trailer.

When he finished his cereal, he returned to the bedroom and flopped on the bed.

What will I tell her?

He snatched Randi's photo once more and sat on the edge of the bed, staring at the picture he grasped firmly in both hands.

I'll just tell her the truth. That I'm a jerk who doesn't deserve her. It'll at least be a relief not to have to lie to her anymore.

Ben sighed and lifted his head slightly. He noticed the bottle of aspirin his father had left on the desk.

"Whoa," he said aloud. "Can't be too careful." He set Randi's picture down on the bed, palmed the aspirin bottle and walked to the bathroom. He stood over the toilet and calculated the number of doses he should have taken. He shook the tablets into his palm and dumped them into the toilet, which he then flushed.

He probably won't notice whether I took them or not, he admitted, *but just in case.*

He returned to his room and set the aspirin bottle back on the desk. He stood for a moment at the desk, motionless. Then, suddenly, he checked the time and began to dress.

When he was fully dressed, he went to the kitchen once more, scooped the cereal bowl and spoon from the table and dropped them into the sink. He grabbed the bread wrapper containing half a loaf of bread from the cabinet over the kitchen sink.

Can't stay long, Ben figured as he closed the trailer door behind him and headed for Spring Park. *Just an hour or so. An hour would be safe.*

Spring Park was less than a mile from Ben's trailer court. It wasn't much of a park, really. Just a pond surrounded by rocks and trees. But Ben liked the isolation it offered from buildings and roads and cars.

He chose a shaded rock at the pond's edge and sat down. A few ducks paddled warily around the rock. He opened the bread wrapper, took out a couple pieces of the bread and began tearing off fragments and tossing them to the ducks. He threw the first pieces out to the ducks, but drew them gradually closer to him by tossing the bread nearer and nearer to the water at his feet.

When the bread was gone, he shoved the wrapper into his jeans pocket, drew his legs up close to him and wrapped his arms around his knees.

Lord, he prayed, *I've made such a mess of things. How'd I let it get this far? I mean, every time I skipped school, I really meant to go back the next day and start all over again. But every day I cut made it harder to go back, until, I don't know, I guess it just got out of control.*

Ben watched one of the ducks investigate a red leaf that floated on the surface of the pond. It nudged the leaf with its bill and then turned away with its bill pointed snobbishly upward.

I just wish there were some way I could start over, Lord. If I'd known it was going to cost me Randi, I'd have gone to school every day. I would never have missed.

He picked a stick out of the dirt and poked it into the pond.

I would've gone out for sports. I'd even have taken extra credit. I'd have been a straight-A student if it would've made the difference.

Ben had been stirring the water, rippling the surface of the pond with the stick, but suddenly he stopped. He let the stick go and watched it ease into the water and out of sight.

The end of next week, she said. He stared at the breeze-blown surface of the water.

This is Wednesday. Seven school days between now and then. That's IF she doesn't start at Verona until the following Monday. He unfolded his legs and stretched them over the water across the rock.

Not enough time, he figured. *Not nearly enough. I've got over a month of work to catch up, and even then I'd still be in freshman classes. And I don't have any friends. Except Charlie. I'd need his help. I hope he's not still mad at me. Yeah, but even then, how can I make myself look popular in less than two weeks?*

A cloud obscured the afternoon autumn sun.

His hand dropped from his mouth. He let it rest on his thigh.

"No way," he said. "Forget it." He pulled his legs

underneath him and sat cross-legged.

I don't have to make homecoming king, though. Just "normal Christian high school student" will do. Which is another thing, probably the main thing. The kids at school all probably think I'm some junkie or hood or something like that. But Randi's going to expect me to at least live up to what I teach in Sunday school.

He hung his head on his chest and clasped his hands behind his neck. He let out a groan.

I can't believe I'm even thinking this. It's crazy. No way.

He shut his eyes and shook his head slowly from side to side.

"Seven days."

He sat. He didn't move. He didn't speak. He barely thought. He heard the birds and the light rustling of the colored leaves in the trees. He felt the bare whisper of the breeze. His mind worked, but his thoughts were not sentences, not even words. His mind was like the wind-rippled surface of the pond, with lines and impressions constantly appearing and disappearing.

Finally, he breathed deeply, unclasped his fingers and straightened his back.

"Seven days," he said. He took another deep breath. "Eleven if you count the weekends . . . *maybe* 11."

He stood, inserting his hands in the back pockets of his jeans.

"It's crazy." He rolled his eyes. "Impossible is what it is."

He turned toward home.

No way is it going to work, he told himself as he left the park. *But it's the only chance I've got. It's either turn my life and reputation around in 11 days, or say goodbye to Randi.*

As he entered the trailer park, he glanced at his watch.

Uh oh. Stayed a lot longer than I'd planned. He began trotting lightly. *Okay, what will I tell Dad if he's home?* He slowed to a walk again. He needed a moment to think. He was only a few trailers away now. He stopped and patted his pockets.

Shoot! If I had my mailbox key, I could get the mail and—hey, what's the difference? I went to get the mail and realized when I got to the office that I forgot my key. That ought to do it.

He started again and walked the few steps to Lot #67. He slowed as he turned the corner of the trailer. His father's car was not in the driveway.

Ben blew a long breath through his pursed lips. "You worry me, Howard," he said to himself. "You're getting awful good at lying."

The music from his room met him as he entered the mobile home. *Forgot to turn it off again,* he thought. He returned to his bedroom and dove onto his rumpled bed.

"I'm *definitely* going back to school tomorrow," he said.

Chapter 10

$\mathcal{H}$e slapped the alarm button on his clock radio and in the same instant that the music stopped, Ben's mind snapped to attention.

It'll never work, he thought glumly. He reviewed yesterday's reasonings and last night's events and wondered, *What ever made me think that I could actually pull this off?* He'd stayed home from the prayer meeting at church to get ready for school. Most of the evening, however, he'd spent trying, without success, to call Charlie Parker to enlist his help.

Now the immensity of his task loomed over him like a monster in a Japanese movie. He felt the cavity opening in his chest again, and he wanted to cry.

He sat on the edge of the bed, elbows on his knees and his face in his hands. *No way.* He sighed, and the hot breath trapped by his hands blew back in his face.

I might as well just stay home today, he reasoned. *Eleven days. There's not enough time. It'll never work.*

His mind stopped forming words and sentences again. He envisioned the next eleven days if he gave up. More cat-and-mouse games with his father, more lying to him and Randi, more, more, more and worst of all, waiting for his world to end when Randi discovered the truth.

He finally struggled to his feet as his father called his name.

"I'm up, Dad."

He trudged through the motions of dressing and washing and brushing and combing and gulping and spooning and combing again until he climbed into the car and rode in silence to school.

As his father dropped Ben off in front of Verona High and drove away, Ben surveyed the stream of students flowing toward him and through the school's glass doors. The sea of strange faces seemed to be arriving in waves, a clump of six or seven dressed mostly in leather, then a huddle of four girls wearing identical eyeglasses. Ben felt unspeakably alone in the teenage traffic. A car horn sounded and he turned. A jumble of arms waved from a foreign sports car, and he squinted to see who was honking and waving at him. A giggling blonde bounded by him. She reached into the car window and withdrew a bundle of schoolbooks. Ben watched as the car lurched and stopped, threading its way back up the school drive.

Lord, he prayed, *I'm gonna need Your help here. I don't know if I can do this.*

As he mouthed the words, he spied one familiar head in the crowd. He ducked and darted through the mass of jeans and jackets that separated him from that head, bobbing like an apple in a water barrel. Finally he reached his objective and thrust his hand out to grab Charlie's arm.

"Charlie! Man, am I glad to see you."

Charlie regarded Ben quickly, then turned back to the others in his small group.

"Catch you guys later," he said.

"Listen," Ben began breathlessly. "I need your help."

Charlie jittered, thrusting his hands in and out of his pockets. "Yeah, well you know, AWOL, how come that doesn't surprise me?"

Ben blinked dumbly at his friend.

"You'll have to get help somewhere else this time, AWOL, 'cause I'm done lettin' you use me."

He whirled and trotted off, leaving Ben standing alone on the emptying sidewalk. He felt like a boxer who leaps from his corner at the start of the first round only to be met with a left, a right and another left that leave him swaying, struggling to keep his feet.

The tardy bell jolted him to the realization that, except for one or two stragglers, he now stood by himself. The crowd had vanished like townspeople from a gunfight in some old movie western.

He entered the building and cast confused looks up and down the main hall.

Homeroom. He drew himself up stiffly and cocked his head. *Homeroom,* he thought with amazement. *Where the heck is my homeroom? He had only attended homeroom once or twice at the very start of the school year, and in each case had slipped out before first period. This is gonna be even harder than I thought,* he lamented. After a moment of indecision, he headed for the school office.

He stepped into the office and was brought short by the assault of sound and activity that met him. A secretary juggled two telephones, punching and repunching an array of flashing buttons on each. A lady, probably a teacher, fed sheets of paper into a kachunking electric stapler. Two students brushed past Ben and out the door, each hugging an armload of paper. A man in a sweatsuit patted a volleyball on the counter as he scribbled on a yellow pad and a thin woman with heavy makeup stood calmly next to him in the center of all the activity like a policeman directing traffic.

Ben stepped tentatively to the counter and planted himself in front of the thin woman.

"Gimme minute, honey," she said and issued instructions on reloading the stapler to the teacher, who grimaced as if in pain.

"Now, honey," she said as she returned her attention to Ben. "What do you need?"

Ben swallowed hard and said, "Uh, ahem, uh . . . I lost my schedule."

"Oh, that all?" she answered. "You mean you haven't written it down anywhere? Land sakes, you should know it by heart I should think, honey. What's your name?"

Ben, dumbfounded momentarily, finally replied, "Uh, Howard. Ben Howard."

"Howard. Ben Howard. You a new student or something? Howard, Howard, Howard," she muttered, picking through a file of multi-colored cards. "Howard. Here y'are." She glanced at the card, then a little uncertainly at Ben. She seemed to shake her uncertainty quickly, though, and handed the card to Ben. "Here y'are, honey. Just run off a copy on that machine and bring it right back to me, 'kay?" She pointed to a copying machine in the corner.

Ben nodded and followed her instructions. He turned to leave the office and then wheeled quickly, remembering something. The thin woman's head was turned from him and when she noticed him back at the counter, she held up an index finger toward him to indicate she'd be with him shortly. He waited until she raised her eyebrows at him and curved her lipstick into a smile.

"Uh, yeah," he said, "I'm sorry to bother you again, but I've also forgotten my, uh, locker combination." He smiled sheepishly at her. "Any way you can give it to me?"

She squinted at him slightly, as if testing his trustworthiness.

" 'Kay," she said after a second, and rummaged in another file. She pulled the card after another mumbled "Howard, Howard, Howard," and extended it to him. Suddenly, though, she withdrew it. "What's your birthday, honey?" He told her.

"Year?"

He told her.

Satisfied, she handed him the card, which he took gratefully. He proceeded to the corner to copy it. When he returned the card, he remained before her, not heading for the door this time.

" 'Kay, what now, honey?" she asked, leaning her elbows on the counter.

"Uh, the locker number's not on here." She stared

at him, open-mouthed. Ben wore an apologetic half-smile and waited what seemed half the day.

"Okay," she said with forced patience, "before I go rummaging through the files again, is there anything else you're going to need?"

Ben shook his head.

Moments later, he sighed heavily as the office door closed behind him. He went to locate his locker.

This is impossible, he told himself. The first period bell rang as he fidgeted with his locker combination. He'd missed homeroom entirely, which meant that he'd need a tardy slip from the attendance office to get into his first class.

The attendance office. He felt like giving up again. *They'll eat me alive*, he thought.

He drew a deep breath, slammed his locker door and set out for the attendance office. *At least I know where that is*, he thought.

He approached the tiny cubicle that was called the attendance "office" and spoke to its inhabitant through the hole in the glass, like he were buying tickets at a theater or withdrawing money from a bank. The woman in the booth barely looked up from her book. She accepted his explanation and slid a green slip of paper under the glass. Ben snatched it thankfully and, with a fumbling glance at his class schedule, reported to his first period: biology.

A hush seized the classroom as Ben entered just before the bell. Mr. Billups was bending over his desk, but straightened at the sudden silence. He blinked at Ben, then grinned widely.

"AWOL!" he exploded.

Terror gripped Ben as Mr. Billups strode to him with extended arms. He hugged Ben dramatically, feigning a kiss on each cheek and draped an arm around Ben's shoulder as he turned him to face the room full of freshman biology students.

"Ladies and gentlemen, we have an honored guest." Mr. Billups could be "corny" sometimes, but most of the students at Verona High appreciated his humor and ranked him as one of their favorite teachers. At this moment, Ben did not.

"Most of you," Billups continued, "come to school because you have to, because your parents make you, because it's the law. But this gentleman is in school today, I assure you, only because he has finally surrendered to his deepest urge . . ."

Here he paused for effect.

". . . to learn about the nervous system!"

Suppressed chuckles mingled with pathetic groans as Billups released his hold and allowed Ben to slink into the only vacant chair in the room.

Mr. Billups proceeded theatrically to announce the lab for the day. A tray containing small silver instruments was distributed to each pair of "lab partners."

"I'm Ben Howard," he whispered to the boy who sat beside him.

"I know," he answered. "You've been my lab partner since the first day of school."

The boy's irritated tone was unmistakable. "Oh," was all Ben could think to say. A larger tray was passed next from table to table. Ben discerned its contents long before the tray reached his table. The students' reactions flowed through the room like

"The Wave" undulating through the stands of a football stadium.

When the tray reached Ben's table, his companion thrust it at him. Gingerly, Ben plucked the odorous preserved frog from the tray and set it on top of the instruments in the smaller tray. He then had to pick the utensils from under the rubbery amphibian like a child playing pickup sticks.

As Billups issued instructions from the front of the room, Ben turned to his partner.

"Well, guess we better get started, huh?"

The boy looked disgustedly at Ben.

"*You* better get started," the boy said.

Ben's face wavered between a look of confusion and amusement at the boy's joke.

"I've had to do all this junk by myself since school started. So you're on your own today."

The boy then faced forward and seemed to fasten his eyes on Billups' form at the front. Ben stared at the side of his partner's face for a moment, then at Billups. Quickly, he palmed the silver implements, realizing that Billups' instructions had advanced to the second or third step.

By whispering to other students in front and behind him, he solicited enough help to catch up with the dissection and completed the day's lab work without the other boy's help. When the bell signaled the end of the first period, Ben gathered himself and warily moved toward Mr. Billups' desk.

He waited while a freshman cheerleader gushed giddily to the teacher about some overwhelming experience of the night before. Ben picked up only occasional words or phrases from her spitfire speech —"mall,"..."video store,"..."*National Geographic*,"— but Mr. Billups nodded understandingly as if she were reciting the Pledge of Allegiance and were getting all the words right. When she finished and bounced out of the room, Mr. Billups turned his gaze slowly toward him. Ben blushed and cleared his throat.

"I wonder," he said, and his voice cracked, making him blush to a deeper shade, "I wonder if I can, uh, get some makeup work from you for the, for, uh, what I've missed."

An expression of shock flashed across Mr. Billups' face, but he suppressed it quickly. A smile slowly spread across his lips. The widening creases around his mouth seemed to cause little ripples to float over his eyes. Ben couldn't tell if the grin indicated pleasure or only skepticism.

"You mean this isn't just a visit?" Billups sounded doubtful. "You plan to come back tomorrow?"

Ben nodded and squeaked out a weak, "Yes."

"Well, this *is* a red-letter day," he said enthusiastically. "Tell you what we'll do, AWOL. You need to hurry or you're going to be late for next period. I'll have a nice little stack of makeup work ready for you first thing in the morning. How's that?"

"No!" Ben blurted. "I mean, well, if I could I'd like to get started tonight."

Mr. Billups leaned back in his swivel chair.

"After all," Ben explained, "I've missed a lot."

Billups tipped his head in agreement. "Well," he said, "you've got that right. Okay. I'll have it for you after school."

The bell rang.

"Thanks," Ben said as he bolted for the door. He started a half-run to his next class, but stopped abruptly as he reached the staircase.

Wait a minute, he reproached himself. *You don't even know where you're going.* He pulled his schedule out. *Second period, second period. There—phys. ed.* His shoulders sagged. *Oh, man, I'm supposed to have gym clothes and everything.*

He gritted his teeth and balled his fists. His face tensed until he erupted with a vehement "Man!" He'd come closer than ever before to using profanity, but at the last moment the word transformed inside his mouth.

"Lord, I can't take this." He glanced around to see if anyone was close enough to hear. *It's only second period and I'm losing the battle. I'm not even sure I can make it through today, never mind turning my life around before Randi comes.*

He had made no conscious decision, but discovered he had started walking toward the gymnasium.

But I know I've got to do it. I don't want Randi to know. I don't want anyone to know what I've been doing.

He opened the gym door.

Just get me through this period, Lord. A mob of guys ascended the locker room steps and muscled by him.

At least tomorrow's Friday.

Chapter 11

Ben fidgeted in the wooden chair outside the guidance counselor's office. The chair was slightly uneven so that he rocked unconsciously from one side to the other and back again while he waited.

It was the first lunch period, but even though he felt a little hungry and weak, he was skipping lunch today to see Mr. McCracken. *Besides*, he argued, *I'm not that hungry. I think I'm just feeling the effects of last night.* He'd arrived home after school Thursday with an armload of makeup work for each of his classes. Yesterday's scene with Billups had been repeated with every teacher except Mr. Henson, the phys. ed. teacher. Ben imagined there really wasn't any way to make up field hockey and running laps, or, if there was, he sure didn't want to do it.

He had jumped into the makeup assignments right away and, except for dinner and an unusually brief phone conversation with Randi, he had stayed with it until about one o'clock in the morning.

That's probably why I feel so crummy. I'm not used to

getting up this early. Well, he allowed, *I guess I am, but I'm used to going back to bed long before now.*

A pair of adult legs passed him, and he raised his glance to see if it was Mr. McCracken. It wasn't; it was some history teacher whose name he didn't know.

Besides, he continued, *I probably sprained my brain or something with all that homework and studying I did last night. No wonder my head feels like a bowling ball. Worst part of it is, I hardly made a dent in all the work I have to do.*

He bent his head over his knees and stared at the floor tiles between his feet. A familiar pair of sneakers entered his vision and stood toe-to-toe with Ben's shoes. He tilted his head back.

"Charlie," he cried and sprang to his feet. Ordinarily Ben would have punched Charlie in the arm or used some other playful gesture of friendship. However, Charlie's outburst yesterday made Ben hesitate. *I know he's pretty upset with me,* he figured, *so I have to be careful.* Unable to decide what to do with his hands, Ben buried them in his pockets.

"Charlie," he repeated uncomfortably, "how's it going?"

Charlie opened his mouth to say something, but both boys were distracted when Mr. McCracken raced around the corner, nearly plowing Charlie over like a bulldozer toppling a tree.

"Whoa, sorry guys," McCracken said as he stopped and steered around them. He disappeared into his office and shut the door behind him.

Ben looked from the door to Charlie and back to the door.

A high-speed courtroom drama enacted itself inside Ben's brain, with himself acting as both prosecution and defense attorneys.

If you came here to see Mr. McCracken, what're you waiting for?

Yeah, but I can't afford to make Charlie any madder. I need him.

You need McCracken, too.

But if I cut him off now, he'll never speak to me.

And if you wait much longer, lunch period will be over. You can't afford to waste any time. You're two years behind to begin with.

"Charlie, man, I'm sorry," he blurted finally. "I've got to go." He turned, fumbled for the doorknob and then remembered to knock.

When he heard a muffled, "Come in," he glanced back at his friend. Charlie's brow was creased and his lips drew a straight line across his face. "Later, okay?" Ben offered as he opened the door.

Once inside, Ben breathed deeply and struggled to clear Charlie Parker from his mind.

"Be with you in a minute," the man said, and Ben crept into one of the molded chairs facing the desk.

I hate this, he thought. The impression was so harsh that he jerked up his head to look at Mr. McCracken, fearful that he had spoken the words out loud. But the guidance counselor continued working.

Ben clenched his teeth in frustration. *I've got a little over a week to "reform" myself before Randi gets here. I have enough makeup work to occupy me 'til Christmas. And my only friend in the whole world is mad at me.*

"Now," Mr. McCracken said. He released his pencil

and plopped his forearms down on the paper-covered desk. "How can I help you?"

Ben scratched his neck.

"Well," he said, his eyes darting from McCracken to the floor in front of his chair and back and forth. "I was wondering if I could change my homeroom and lunch period."

Mr. McCracken turned his palms upward on the desk. "How come?" he said.

Ben's throat tightened. He knew that a big decision was coming up. Like a sharp turn in a road, he saw the sign. He'd tried to plot strategy beforehand, to develop a plan and stick with it. He knew, though, that when the moment came he'd have only a few seconds to choose his course.

"Well, sir," he started cautiously, "I'm in a freshman homeroom and lunch period. I'd like to change. To be in with kids my own age." He swallowed. *Hey, that was pretty good.*

McCracken lifted his arms off the desk and leaned back in his swivel chair, in the old "let's watch the student sweat" posture.

"How old are you?"

"Sixteen," Ben answered.

"What are you doing in a freshman homeroom then?"

"I've, like, flunked most of my courses," he said, adding after a moment, "sir."

The chair creaked as McCracken bent forward on the desktop again. One eyelid drooped in a half wink.

"What's your name?" he asked it as if it had momentarily slipped his mind, not like he'd never known it.

Ben groaned inwardly.

"Howard, sir," he answered. "Ben Howard." The guidance counselor stood and strode from the room. Ben felt roller-coaster flutters in his stomach as he sat in the silent office waiting for Mr. McCracken's return. A sudden light change in the room drew Ben's attention to the single window behind McCracken's desk. The sun had slipped behind a cloud and shadowed the room in an eerie grey shroud. The sensation in his stomach interfered with his breathing, and he thought of giving up and sneaking out. Before he could act, though, McCracken entered the room again, causing Ben to jump when the door he'd elbowed open clanged into the metal bookcase behind Ben's chair.

The tall, balding man rounded the corner of his desk, slapped the file folder on the open palm of his left hand as he held it in his right, and said, "You've hardly attended a day of school in the last two years."

"Yes, sir, I know." His voice quivered. McCracken stared thoughtfully at Ben as he stuck his chin out and began scraping the stubble on his neck with the edge of the file folder.

"I don't get it." He sat down. "Why do you need to change homeroom and lunch period now? You're still going to have to take freshman classes. What's the point?"

This is it, Ben thought. *What am I going to do?* He could lie, of course. *You see, Mr. McCracken, last week I had a religious experience that made me see the error of my ways. So I've come back to school not only to make up for*

*lost time, but to share my good fortune with other sixteen-
year-olds.*

He knew that would never work. He'd considered
something like, *My psychiatrist says I've come a long way
and that I'm ready to cope with school again, but that
developing relationships with kids my own age is necessary
for a full recovery.*

He dismissed that approach, too.

Could tell the truth, he admitted. *It's like this, Mr.
McCracken. I'm a Christian, but for the last two years I've
lived a double life. I've been a perfect Christian teenager at
church, really I have, and not just pretending or putting
up a front but honest and sincere about my commitment to
Christ. But as far as school stuff goes, I've messed up. I've
skipped school, I've lied to my teachers, to my dad, to
everybody at church.*

Ben knew he couldn't say all that to McCracken.
Mostly, he thought, *because he might think all Christians
are as phony as I've been. He might think that my life at
church is a lie, but it's everywhere else that I've been living
a lie. The way I feel about Christ is real, but he'd never see
it that way.*

"Mister Howard," McCracken still stared at Ben.
"Are you going to say anything?"

Ben suddenly felt tired. He made several false starts
before he gushed, "My girlfriend is transferring here
in a week." He stared at the chipped edge of the desk.
He knew Mr. McCracken was looking at him, but he
couldn't meet his eyes. "She doesn't know that I'm
still a freshman, and I'm afraid that when she finds
out, she won't . . ." He stopped. When he spoke again,
his voice barely emerged beyond his own lips. "I'm

afraid she'll drop me," he continued. "So, if I can get into a junior homeroom and lunch period . . ." His voice trailed off and he lowered his gaze to his clammy hands pinched between his knees.

Ben felt McCracken's silent stare upon him. He still could not force himself to look at the man behind the desk, and neither of them broke the awkward quiet in the room. McCracken seemed to be waiting for him to go on, but Ben wrestled uselessly to find something more to say that would help his case.

Finally, the guidance counselor stood and walked from behind the desk out of the office again. Ben rubbed his eyes fretfully and then scanned the furnishings of the room. The bookcase behind Ben's chair displayed boring titles and plain covers. The walls were hung with diplomas and certificates and pictures of people taken a long time ago. Stacks of papers and forms and envelopes littered the surface of the desk and on top, like a twig of parsley on a plate of food, lay the manila folder which contained Ben's school records.

McCracken returned, with another file in his hand. He sat behind his desk, flipping page after page over the top of the folder. Ben noticed they were stapled at one corner.

"The only junior homeroom with any room at all is Miss Bradley's," he began. He leaned his elbows on the desktop and held the folder open in a V between him and Ben. "I suppose I could put you in there."

Ben allowed himself a smile.

"I'd really appreciate that," he said sincerely, and thought again to add, "sir."

"Give this to Miss Bradley on Monday," he said, scribbling a message on a pad. He ripped off the top sheet and handed it to Ben.

"Lunch period is a different matter. Do you have your schedule with you?"

Ben fumbled in his books and extracted the tattered piece of paper.

"See," Mr. McCracken said as he consulted the schedule, "moving you to a later lunch period would involve a schedule change and class change and all that goes with it." He looked up from the paper. "And to be honest with you, I'm not going to go that far out of my way for you. Not right now, anyway. Maybe after you've knuckled down and shown me some effort." He returned the schedule.

Ben wore a worried look. *By that time*, he argued inwardly, *it'll be too late.*

Mr. McCracken glanced at his watch. "You'll need a pass to get back in your class." He began jotting another note on the pad.

Ben recognized the tone of dismissal in McCracken's words. He stood, juggling his books momentarily before regaining a firm grasp. He reached out for the pass, but McCracken withheld it.

"Now, I've done you a favor," he said, holding the pass. "You do a favor for me."

Ben nodded. McCracken held his eyes with a gaze that would not allow him to look away.

"Stop using your intelligence to con people," he said with no trace of humor or softness in his voice, "and start using it to make something of yourself."

They locked eyes for a moment longer, until Mr.

McCracken extended the piece of paper to Ben. He muttered a "thank you" and took the pass. He turned when he reached the door. McCracken still watched him.

"Thanks again," Ben said, and glided out into the hall. He paused at the foot of the staircase to think. He had succeeded in changing homerooms, but he would still have to eat with freshmen. Randi would wonder about that. *How will I explain it?* he questioned. No answer came to his mind. He shrugged. *I'll think of something. I'll have to.*

He began to climb the stairs, but halted abruptly.

"Where am I going?" he said out loud. He rolled his eyes and dug out the rumpled schedule again.

Chapter 12

$\mathcal{P}$ain pierced Ben's side like the jab of a knife between his ribs.

He summoned his will and, with a teeth-gritting grunt, rolled on his belly to escape the pain. Immediately, though, a sharp point plunged into his chest and he recoiled again.

He sat up and, with bloodshot eyes, faced the source of his torment. He rubbed his wounded side with one hand as he started to clear his book-strewn bed with the other.

He groaned repeatedly as he gathered the books into a stack on the floor. He rubbed his face and peered at the clock radio from under puffy eyelids. The red numbers seemed to waver like heat shimmering off a summer pavement. He blinked both eyes at once. The numbers blinked in response: 9:30.

"Nine thirty," he said. He groaned again. *At least it's Saturday. How late was I up last night?* He fought to remember but had only an impression that he had studied until after 2:30 in the morning.

"I'm killing myself," he said. "That's what I'm doing, I'm killing myself."

He dragged himself through the motions of showering and dressing, finally settling at his cluttered desk with a bowl of cereal and a glass of orange juice. He filled his chest with air and held it for a moment before exhaling.

"Okay. Where was I?" He transferred the stack of books from beside the bed back onto the desk. "I guess biology is as good as anything." He took a mouthful of cereal and flipped the pages of his biology text.

The cereal bowl and juice glass were empty when Ben's father knocked later that morning.

"Got a minute, son?"

"Sure, Dad."

Mr. Howard sat on the bed. Ben turned in his chair to face his father. Little more than a foot separated their faces in the confines of the tiny bedroom.

"Ben, I know that I've been absorbed in work the last couple of weeks and haven't really much . . . been around for you." Even without his father's struggling for words, Ben sensed his discomfort. "But I wanted you to know, son, I just wanted to say, that I've noticed how hard you've been hitting the books lately and, I'm, uh, really proud of you."

A few moments passed before he realized his father was finished. Both pairs of eyes floated nervously around the room like houseflies, never lighting on any surface for more than a second.

"Well, thanks Dad, I, uh . . ." Ben's voice trailed off and he gathered himself to repeat. "Thanks."

His father hesitated on the edge of the bed, like the split second when a student realizes that his cafeteria chair has been pulled out from beneath him, before he plunges to the floor. Ben hesitated, too, pondering for a moment whether he should confess to his father what he'd been doing for the last two years and tell him how things had changed now. He wanted to respond to his dad's tenderness and honesty, but finally it was that tenderness that closed Ben's mouth as his father excused himself awkwardly from the room.

I can't tell him now, he decided. *Not when he's just finished telling me how proud he is of me. Besides,* he reasoned as he turned back to his homework, *telling him now would start a long discussion and I'd have to explain a lot of things and I don't have time for all that right now, not with all this makeup work to do and only five days of classes left, before Randi starts at Verona. Besides, I also need to get tight again with Charlie.*

"Charlie!" He lifted his head and looked at his reflection in the mirror over the desk. "What am I going to do about Charlie?"

He sprang from his desk and went to the phone. Charlie's grandmother answered and, recognizing Ben's voice, started to turn from the phone to call Charlie. Ben stopped her.

"No, don't call him to the phone. If it's okay with you, I'll come over."

He jammed the phone down and rocketed out the door. Moments later he was on the steps of Charlie's trailer.

Charlie opened the door before Ben knocked.

"Hi," he said, unsmiling.

"Can we talk?"

Charlie leaned back into the room to tell his grandmother he was going out. He closed the door behind him and sat on the top step as Ben retreated to the pavement in front of the steps.

"Look," Ben started. "I'm really sorry for everything that's happened the last couple days. I know I've been a lousy friend and I want to make it up to you any way I can."

Charlie propped himself back on his arms which were extended behind him like an inverted V. Ben went on to explain the reason for his behavior recently, relating Randi's excited announcement at Mama's Pizza, his wild scheme to remake himself before next weekend, what he'd already started and all that remained to be done. Charlie's eyes widened as Ben talked.

"You're crazy," he said when Ben finished.

"I know," Ben admitted.

They both fell silent for a few seconds until finally Ben drooped his head.

"Anyway, Charlie, I'm really sorry. And I'll make it up to you."

"Yeah." Charlie stood. A crooked smile crossed his face and he wagged his head as if to shake off the apology. "Doin' anything tonight?"

Ben shoved his hands into his pockets. "Just cramming, I guess."

"How about going to Dan Collins' party with me?"

Ben started to refuse, thinking of all the homework he had to do, but he checked himself. He'd just promised to make it up to Charlie. Maybe this was the way to do it. And Dan Collins was a senior, one of the most popular.

"What time?"

"Nine o'clock sound good?"

"Nine o'clock?"

"I'll see if Uncle Bill will let me use his car."

Ben agreed and walked back to his trailer. He wasn't sure this was such a good idea, but he put his misgivings aside and determined to start his personal popularity campaign that night at Dan Collins' house.

The afternoon passed neither quickly nor slowly. Ben alternated between biology, English, algebra and American history for most of the afternoon. At one point he nearly fell asleep on his history book but caught himself before he began to drool on the pages. He called Randi for a brief conversation, heading back to his desk when he hung up. He called her again that evening, but the second call was shorter than the first because it was interrupted by Charlie honking to pick Ben up for the party.

The parked cars and droning music indicated Dan Collins' house. Light shone from every window and the music seemed loud even from the end of the driveway. They paused just inside the front door, which was propped open by a large glass cat. The brisk evening air outside surrendered to the smoky stuffy atmosphere which hung inside the house like the dark velvet drapes in funeral home windows.

Ben shouted into Charlie's ears, "Where are Dan's parents?"

Charlie responded with a shrug as he surveyed the

mess of teenagers, some of whom looked older than high school age. They made their way to the refreshments in the kitchen, which seemed limited to several varieties of beer and chips. Someone had made an attempt at some kind of red punch, so Ben and Charlie located two paper cups that appeared unused in the litter of discarded cups and plates on the table and counters. They had less luck finding clean plates, so they each grabbed a handful of chips and wandered through the party balancing a punch cup in one hand and eating chips from the other. They spoke infrequently, and then only to each other.

They stood at the foot of the staircase watching kids file up and down. Ben thought, *I'm sure I don't want any part of what's going on up there.* He was distracted from the staircase by a football player guzzling beer in the next room. *I don't want any part of what's going on down here, either.* He turned to Charlie and started to speak, but then simply grabbed his arm and pulled him aside, into the dining room.

"Charlie, I don't like this party."

Charlie looked like he was about to agree when he stopped. His mouth hung open and his eyes pointed to the front door. As Ben turned that direction, he was suddenly aware of a voice raised above the din of the party. Before he could follow Charlie's gaze to the source of interest, he felt Charlie yanking him in the other direction into the kitchen.

"What?" Ben questioned his friend loudly when they stood together, almost alone in the kitchen. "What?" he repeated. "What's up?"

"Cops," Charlie shouted, wild-eyed. "We've got to

get outta here."

They each whirled around in the room like cornered cats.

"Where's the back?"

"I don't know," Charlie answered. "I've never been here before."

Charlie opened a pantry door in the kitchen. Ben bounded around the corner and tried another door.

"Charlie," he shouted above the music. "Here!"

They raced together down the basement steps as the music snapped off overhead. The staircase plunged into darkness.

"Is there a way out down here?" Charlie's voice was a harsh whisper.

"How am I supposed to know?"

The two fumbled in darkness for a light switch. Charlie located a door, opened it and whispered to Ben.

"I think it's the garage."

Ben dashed to Charlie's side and followed him into the dark garage. Ben fumbled frantically up and down the wall beside the door searching for a switch. Footsteps thundered ominously in the rooms above. His fingers finally located something on the wall and at the same moment the garage door began to lift noisily. Ben and Charlie turned panicked faces to each other. They said nothing but both bolted for the yawning doors at the same instant.

They sprinted across the lawn to the six-foot wooden privacy fence that encircled the yard. They vaulted the fence and landed together on the other side, Ben on all fours and Charlie on one knee. Barely

95

pausing, they stood again and darted to escape this backyard they now occupied.

They'd hardly taken three steps when they sank into a shallow pond which covered their ankles. Breathing expressions of disgust and frustration, they stepped out of the water and, more carefully but quickly (spurred on by the barking of a not-too-distant dog), skirted the house and arrived on the sidewalk.

Ben doubled over, his legs straight with his hands on his knees like a sprinter who's just finished a race. Charlie glanced around until he gained his bearings.

"Come on," he said.

Ben followed his friend and together they squished down the street, around the corner and up the next street until they reached Charlie's parked car.

Chapter 13

"Nobody saw us Saturday night, so we're cool."

Ben peered around his locker door at Charlie. "What?"

"Nobody saw us," Charlie repeated. "Turns out the cops didn't really do much. Dan's brother was there and he kind of took responsibility. The cops just made 'em turn the music off and sent everybody home. No big thing."

Ben's face was expressionless.

"Oh."

"As far as I can tell, though, nobody saw us slip out the way we did." Charlie chattered like a bird in a pet store. "Be pretty embarrassing if anyone saw us. Bet we looked kind of dumb."

"Yeah," Ben replied. He clanged his locker door and spun the combination lock. They walked down the hall together until Charlie slapped Ben on the shoulder, spat a few automatic words of parting and ducked into his first period classroom.

Ben continued down the hall and up the stairs.

"It figures," he muttered as he hurried to biology class. *Dan Collins' party didn't do me a bit of good. I didn't make any new friends, didn't talk to anybody. I bet nobody even noticed I was there. Unless . . . ,* he thought as he slipped into Billups' room just ahead of the bell, *yeah, it'd be just my luck if somebody did see me and Charlie sneaking out the garage and landing in that fish pond or whatever it was.*

He opened a notebook and started doodling, heedless of what Billups was saying at the chalkboard.

Lord, I really feel like You ought to be helping me more than this. The harder I try, it seems things keep getting worse, not better. His mind replayed his embarrassment yesterday. He had completely forgotten to prepare for his Sunday school class until he grabbed his Bible to head out to the car. He had tried to work on the lesson during the drive to church, but he felt like it was obvious to everyone that he hadn't studied.

Randi especially, he reflected. *She acted a little funny all day. She must sense something's wrong.*

His pencil point snapped off.

Stop it, Howard. You're being paranoid. He peeled the pencil at the tip to expose the lead so he could write with it. It was his only pencil. *She can't suspect anything yet. That'll come soon enough,* he thought gloomily.

He tested the pencil. *Almost.* He chipped off a little more. *There,* he decided as the pencil wrote smoothly again.

Billups was drawing on the chalkboard and spouting something about the circulation system being like army supply lines to troops in the Civil War. Ben started to listen but his thoughts were soon drawn back to his dilemma.

Next step, he figured, *is to sign up for some sport or something so I can look involved.* His doodling started to take the shape of a list.

Football. He hesitated a moment. *Nope, too late.* He scratched an "X" through the word.

Okay. He made another entry to his list. *Baseball.* He crossed that out almost immediately. *Too early.*

He considered for a moment and started to write, "Basketball." He scribbled it out, too. *Yeah, sure. Whose shoulders are you going to stand on?*

This is getting me nowhere. He considered every sport that sprang to mind. *Track. Cross country. Soccer.* He eliminated each. *Too late, too early, not fast enough, not big enough.*

He ripped the page from his notebook just as the bell signaled the end of first period. Billups held his palm up like a traffic cop and halted the class until he'd barked the homework assignment. Ben closed the notebook around the pencil and started out the door. At the top of the staircase he halted, spun and entered Billups's room again. He dug in his notebook, extracted a page of makeup work and handed it to the teacher with a few hasty words of explanation. That done, he left the room again and started his trek to the far end of the school building for his physical education class.

Three hours later as he finished his lunch, he mourned his inability to think of a sport or club he could join to help his mission.

There's got to be something, he thought. He sat beside

a freshman who finger-poked his glasses higher on his nose after nearly every bit of food. Ben watched him. He lowered his face toward the plate, the glasses slipped down his nose, he took a bite, lifted his head and, as he chewed, returned his glasses to their original position against his forehead.

Ben shook his head. *Freshmen,* he thought. An idea occurred to him. He inspected the chewing freshmen as the thought developed in his mind. He examined the stack of books beside the boy's tray.

Harold Baker. He read the penciled name on one of the books.

"Harold," he said out loud.

The boy poked his glasses again and peered through them at Ben. Doubt showed on his face.

"You talking to me?" he asked.

"Your name's Harold, isn't it?"

The boy looked at Ben as if he were speaking a foreign language. "Yeah," he replied after a moment's hesitation.

"Well, listen, Harold. You play any sports?" Ben scratched the back of his head. "Belong to any clubs? Here at school, I mean."

"No." Harold blinked at Ben like he'd just been accused of selling secrets to the Soviets. "Well," he added, "no sports. I, well, I guess I do help out a little bit on the yearbook staff."

"Oh, yeah?" Ben's interest encouraged the boy.

"Yeah, I'm, well, I'm not really on the yearbook staff, but Mrs. Peters likes me, sort of, and she, well, I just kind of help her."

"Oh."

"I'm the only boy on the staff, even though, well, like I said, I'm not really on the staff."

"Yeah," Ben answered. *Thought I had something there for a minute,* he thought. *Oh, well, I haven't even looked at a yearbook since eighth grade, probably. I would barely know what's in a yearbook. Everybody's picture, I know that, but beyond that, what? All the teams, football and baseball teams, and all that, I guess. Clubs, too. Spanish clubs, stuff like that.* The thought surprised him.

"Yeah," he said. "Stuff like that. Clubs."

He sprang suddenly to his feet, prompting Harold to flinch, as if Ben were about to punch him. He disposed of his lunch and, with a calculating glance at the cafeteria clock, dashed out the side door. He hesitated only a moment before he remembered where the school library was.

He wound up and down the aisles of books in the library, searching for a shelf of Verona High yearbooks. He wandered from the fiction section to a dark corner filled with encyclopedias and research books. He scanned the periodical section and almost picked up a teen magazine with a cover boasting an article, "Six Ways to Save Your Grades!"

Remember why you're here, stupid, he scolded himself. He stood in the periodical section and surveyed the library.

"I give up," he said and strolled over to the counter in the middle of the room. He positioned himself between the two cardboard signs labeled, "Book Checkout" and "Book Return."

"Hi," he said. The girl behind the counter raised her eyes from the book in her lap.

"Oh, hi," she answered. Long red hair framed her dainty features.

Wow, Ben thought. *She's nice looking.* The redhead waited. She closed her book and straightened her legs from the rung of the stool beneath her.

Concentrate, stupid, he reminded himself. "Umm," he stalled, and then remembered, "Oh yeah, I need a yearbook. You know, last year's yearbook would do, I guess."

The girl turned to the bookcase behind her, pulled a book and held it toward Ben.

"Is that all you need?"

Ben hesitated for a second before answering. "Yeah. Thanks. Can I check this out?"

"Nope, sorry. It has to stay in the library."

"Oh." Ben checked his watch. "Okay. Thanks." With another glance at his watch, he turned from the counter and made his way to a table. He sat and began thumbing the pages of the yearbook.

After a few moments he clucked his tongue in disgust. He had flipped from front to back, turned the book over into his other hand and flipped from back to front without any of the pages registering on his mind.

This is crazy, he thought. *My brain is like putty today.* He started flipping pages again, slowly. *Now concentrate. Clubs. Sports and clubs.*

"Sports and clubs," he repeated, out loud this time. He paused when he reached the title page labeled with a diagonal "SPORTS," but he soon turned the last page of that section with no new inspiration.

A moment later he found the section of the book

which listed clubs and activities. The pages fell in rhythms now, one by one, Spanish Club, French Club, Russian Club. Frustration began to rise in him. Chess Club, Drama Club, School newspaper, Yearbook staff. He knew he was about to run out of pages and opportunities. Suddenly he froze.

"Wait a minute," he whispered. He hurriedly turned back, two pages, three pages. *There.* He stared at the page thoughtfully. *Drama club.*

He lay the book open on the table.

Drama club. His mouth hung open as he pondered. "Yeah," he said. "That might do it." He scooted his chair loudly away from the table, leaned back, stretched his legs and crossed one ankle atop the other.

"Drama club," he repeated. "I bet I could do that." He drummed his fingers on the book. "I've never done it before, but I bet I'd be good at acting."

Yeah, everybody thinks that. Everybody thinks he can act. But I really think I'd be good.

A thought occurred to him. *I've probably had more practice at acting these last two years than anybody in the drama club, that's for sure. I've become so good at lying,* he decided privately, *that I could probably play any part.*

He stood just as the bell rang. He glanced at his watch reflexively and returned the yearbook to the girl at the counter.

He'd turned and stepped away from the counter when he remembered something and whirled. She was sliding the book into place on the shelf.

"Oh, can I see that again?" he asked. "Just for a second."

She withdrew the yearbook once more. He looked

at her apologetically.

"I just want to see who the teacher for the drama club is," he explained as he took the book.

"Oh," she said brightly, "you mean the advisor? Miss Bullard?"

"Well, yeah. That's who it is? Miss Bullard?"

"She's the best. She thinks I ought to study drama in college, like at UCLA or someplace like that."

He held the unopened book.

"You're in the drama club?"

She smiled. "Uh huh," she answered cheerily. "We're open to more people joining, if you're interested. We're just now getting *really* started and it's going to be a lot of fun. You going to join? We could really use more guys."

He studied her bright eyes that illumined a perfect face. *This might be fun,* he thought. He momentarily forgot the clock and his next class and his frantic fight to save his relationship with Randi. He smiled, extended the book to the girl and leaned forward with his elbows on the counter.

"My name's Ben," he said.

Chapter 14

$\mathcal{B}$en awoke Tuesday morning with a sick feeling in the pit of his stomach. He groaned.

"Circle day," he said, and groaned again.

He'd been dreading this day since he began his "Project AWOL," as Charlie had begun calling it.

Tuesday, he reminded himself. *The Circle meets at lunch.*

"The Circle" was the somewhat ordinary name of the group of Christian kids that met every Tuesday during the first lunch period. The Circle was so called because everyone in the group carried their lunches to one corner of the school lawn and sat down in a circle for a short Bible study and discussion.

He hauled his worry through the morning. The knot in his stomach tightened with each bell that tolled the end of one period or the beginning of another.

It had to work this way, didn't it? he grumbled to himself. *If McCracken had let me change lunch periods, everything would've worked out.* The Circle only met during the first lunch.

I could've explained to Randi that I haven't been able to be a part of the Christian group at school because I'm in the wrong lunch period and hardly get to see any of those people. But now, he lamented, *here I am with three more days of school to go before "The End," and only one Circle meeting to get acquainted and start building a Christian reputation.*

He swallowed the lump in his throat and sighed hugely as the clanging of the lunch bell signaled the dreaded hour. He dragged himself from his second floor classroom to the cafeteria and then out to the school lawn with his lunch. With every step, he devised excuses that would allow him to escape this awkward moment. Part of him wanted to avoid the possible embarrassment at any cost and part of him knew that this had to be done if he was going to keep from losing Randi.

By the time he trudged to the meeting place, Ben discovered that the circle had already been formed. He looked around the tight halo of faces without recognizing anyone. Some of the cross-legged students already had Bibles open on their laps. An agonizing moment crawled by while Ben stood outside the circle with his lunch in his hands, looking dumbly at the faces staring wordlessly back at him.

"Uh, hum," Ben cleared his throat. "Have room for me?"

A few clumsy comments rose from the group as the circle of bodies parted and a space on the grass cleared for him. He set his lunch down in front of him and began to eat self-consciously. He tried to lift his head occasionally from his lunch and nod or smile, but his mind whirred like the blades of a helicopter.

They're all looking at me, he thought. Lifting his eyes, he glanced at a few people. Each of them yanked their eyes away a split second before he looked at them.

They're all looking at me, all right, he determined. *They don't seem to be too thrilled to have me here.*

The bodies seated on the grass seemed unnaturally stiff and uncomfortable to Ben.

I probably should say something. Contribute to the Bible study. At least look like I'm listening.

He struggled to look interested in what was being said by the student who appeared to be the leader, but moments later nervous thoughts began darting around his head like the silver sphere of a pinball machine as it ricochets off the bumpers.

This is stupid, he thought. *This'll probably do me about as much good as Dan Collins' party Saturday night. Nobody's shaken my hand or slapped me on the back or introduced themselves to me.*

The leader seemed to be wrapping up the Bible study, like it was almost over.

Randi's gonna come to school next week and probably meet some of these people and find out they're Christians and mention me and they're gonna say, "Who's Ben Howard? He go to this school? He's a Christian? I've never met him, and I thought I knew all the Christians in the place."

Everybody around the circle stood up suddenly, and Ben imagined his opportunity to be disappearing. He stood with them and summoned his courage.

"Uh, my name's Ben Howard," he blurted, "and I really enjoyed this."

Every set of eyes in the group gazed at Ben with an expression of wonder and amazement. A moment of silence followed. Ben scanned the expressions around the group. He felt hot redness rise in his face.

"Thanks," said the student who had led the study. He looked at every face in the circle, as if waiting for more comments. "Now, let's pray," he said at last.

Eyes closed around the circle, and Ben closed his eyes and bowed his head with the others. The redness in his face extended to his neck and threatened to choke off his air.

Oh, great, he moaned inwardly. *They were all standing to pray. They probably do it the same way every time, finish the Bible study and then stand in a circle and pray and I had to go and pick that time to say my piece and make a total jerk out of myself. Now they'll be able to say to Randi, "Oh, you mean the guy who made a fool out of himself last Tuesday at the Circle?" Yeah, this really did a lot of good, Ben.*

Ben realized that the leader must have finished praying when he sensed the circle around him begin to evaporate. He jerked his head up as if waking from a dream. The guy who had led the study stood beside him.

"Hi," he said.

"Hi," Ben answered.

"My name's Ted Cooper," he said. "You'll have to excuse the others. They didn't mean to be unfriendly or anything, it's just that, well, you really surprised them by coming to the Circle."

"Oh," Ben responded.

"I mean, you know, it's like you're the last person they ever expected to see in the Circle."

Ben tilted his head like a dog hearing a high-pitched noise. "Yeah?"

Ted changed the subject. "When did you become a Christian?"

"Well, that's hard to explain. I've been a Christian a while, but I've been going through a hard time."

Ted eyed him suspiciously. "We ought to be going back inside."

They walked together back into the building and parted inside the door. Ben stood for a moment watching Ted walk away from him. Then, in a decisive moment, he called to him.

"Ted!"

He turned.

"Wait up a minute."

Ben jogged the few steps to where Ted waited.

"You said I was the last person they all expected to see in the Circle. What did you mean?"

"Oh, I don't know. Just your . . ." He hesitated. "Just your reputation, I guess."

Ben looked at him, unblinking. "What? You mean the school I've missed?" He thought he was beginning to understand.

"That's part of it, I guess."

Ben understood. He sighed. "What else?"

"Now, I don't know you, Ben. I don't know if it's all true or not." Ben waited. "But your reputation is, you're sort of a junkie. Some people even say you sell the stuff." He stopped again. "Like I said, I don't know how much of it is true, but you know . . ."

That's what I thought, Ben said to himself. *I should have expected it, especially when they all treated me like I had two heads or something.*

The bell rang. Ben grasped Ted's arm just above the elbow and held it.

"Listen, Ted, I can't explain it all to you now. But I'm not a junkie. Like I said, I've kind of been going through a hard time, but I'm not a junkie. And I'm *certainly* not a pusher. Will you tell that to everybody in the Circle?"

Ted smiled sincerely at Ben.

"Yeah, sure," he said. He started to shuffle to his next class, but turned after a few steps. "See ya, Ben."

Ben smiled and nodded after Ted, but when Ted turned around again, Ben's smile disappeared. He felt suddenly tired.

The bell rang again, indicating that Ben was late for his next class. Still, he stood motionless in the hallway outside the cafeteria. Ted's words seemed to echo in the corridor.

Your reputation is, you're sort of a junkie. Some people even say you sell the stuff.

I guess I never realized, he thought, *how hard a thing it is to change your reputation once people have learned to think of you in a certain way. I've never acted like a Christian at school, and it's not like I can go around wearing a sign around my neck that says, "BULLETIN: BEN HOWARD IS NOT A JUNKIE NOR HAS HE EVER BEEN ONE. HE'S A CHRISTIAN, EVEN THOUGH HE HASN'T ACTED LIKE ONE."*

Ben looked up and down the empty hall.

It's so hopeless. My reputation isn't going to change in two weeks. I can go to classes and join the Circle and be in the drama club, but I can't keep Randi from meeting all the people who've seen the way I've been the last couple years.

He contemplated the empty hall.

I could duck out now and go home and no one would see me. I could forget about all this. No more makeup work. No more running around trying to change my reputation overnight. No more Billups, no more McCracken, no more Henson. He hesitated only a second, but one more thought came, unbidden, into his mind. *No more Randi.* He stood for a moment as still as a deer caught in headlights.

Then, slowly, his jaw clenched and his lips tightened into a thin, straight line.

He turned toward his next class.

Chapter 15

With the dismissal bell that heralded the end of the school day, Verona High School seemed to discharge students like a violent sneeze from a fat man. Ben leaned on his locker door and watched as the school emptied and the halls fell quiet. A few students still walked here and there, but the atmosphere had changed suddenly, almost magically—as if the sneezing fat man were settling into a hammock with a satisfied sigh.

Ben realized he'd never seen the school from this perspective. Students in the halls no longer ran as though late for a class, but seemed almost to skip to wherever they were headed. Teachers, too, seemed different.

They look more like real people, he realized, *like when you see your pastor in the supermarket.*

He closed the locker door and headed for Room 121, feeling like he was walking in a dream. He stopped outside the door, smoothed and straightened his hair with his hand, then stepped over the threshold.

Everything in the room seemed to halt in mid-motion. The shrill sound of a girl's laughter stopped abruptly between "tee" and "hee." Two guys in chairs by the door looked up from the paper they were sharing and fastened their eyes on Ben. Miss Bullard choked back the rest of the sentence she had been speaking and joined the staring throng of students.

Deja vu, Ben thought. *This feels like the Circle all over again.* Smiling stiffly, he located the redheaded girl from the library. She smiled back.

Ben introduced himself to Miss Bullard, who turned him by the shoulders to face the others in the room and repeated the same words they'd just heard him tell her.

"I've just been giving out some of the parts, Ben," she explained as he took a seat close to the redhead. "But there's still room for more Thespians." She crooned the last word as though it were a secret between her and the drama club.

He listened attentively as Miss Bullard proceeded to serenade the group with a lilting list of rules and guidelines and "words of wisdom."

After the meeting, which only lasted about half an hour, Ben leaned toward the redhead. She was arranging papers in a notebook and her hair cascaded around her face like a silk curtain.

"Angie," he said softly. He'd learned her name Monday in the library.

She looked up at him, throwing her hair over a shoulder as she turned. She didn't speak, but the expression on her face indicated a response.

He noticed her milky complexion and immediately

became conscious of his blemish-dotted face. He self-consciously lifted a hand to his hair and smoothed it over his forehead.

"Any good parts left?" he asked. She hesitated for a moment.

"Well," she said. She looked like she was thinking. "I don't know. Miss Bullard has the list."

"Yeah," Ben answered agreeably. "Sure, I'll ask her." Angie stood and cradled her books in her arms.

"Do you have your part?" he asked.

She shook her head up and down. He waited for her to speak. She nodded her head again.

"Dorothy," she said. She turned abruptly, flicked her hair out of her way and skipped out of the room.

Dorothy? Ben thought, as he watched her leave. He realized then that he hadn't yet asked what play they were doing. He searched his memory for a clue. *Miss Bullard must have referred to the play in her little speech.* He couldn't recall.

Okay, then, he reasoned. *What shows have a Dorothy in the cast?* He pondered only a moment when it came to him. *The Wizard of Oz.* At the same instant, several comments Miss Bullard had made fell into place, and he knew his deduction was correct.

He turned his gaze to Angie's empty seat. *She's the lead.*

He wanted more than ever now to nab a good part. He walked to Miss Bullard's desk, noting with surprise as he did that they were the only people left in the room.

She purred a few words of welcome to him, telling him how much he was going to enjoy drama club. He asked, when she paused for breath, if there were any parts left for him.

"Well," she began warily. Her hesitation made Ben feel like he was being a little pushy.

"I mean, you know," he added hastily, "I realize you don't know if I can act or anything like that. I mean, like, are there any parts I can try out for?"

"Of course, Ben," she said, smiling like a mother whose child has just said "please."

She lifted a bundle of papers and drew out a stapled stack.

"It so happens we do have a major part we haven't cast yet." She thumbed through the papers in her hand without looking up as she spoke. "Wait just a minute and I'll find it for you."

Ben's insides fluttered. *Major part? I wonder what she means by "major?"* He searched his memory. His excitement grew as he remembered. *The Tin Man. Or Scarecrow. The Cowardly Lion, maybe. What else? The Wizard, but he only appears at the end. That still wouldn't be too bad.* Miss Bullard seemed to have found what she sought. *This could be fun*, Ben thought.

"Here you are, Ben," she said, pointing to a line on the page. "Start reading here. I'll read Dorothy's part. Give me just a minute to find it in my script."

Ben waited. She finally muttered, "There," and motioned for him to read.

He started reading aloud, but then stopped abruptly. He looked at Miss Bullard, then back to the page, and back to Miss Bullard.

"Em?" he said. "My name is Em?"

"*Aunt* Em, Ben," she answered. "*Aunt* Em. You're

Dorothy's aunt."

"Dorothy's aunt?" He stared dumbly at Miss Bullard. She still smiled that motherly smile. Ben swallowed.

"A girl's part?" he said.

"I realize you may not want to try it," Miss Bullard said, "but it *is* a major part."

He looked at her with his mouth hanging open and then looked down at the script again.

"You want me to play a girl." It wasn't a question. Ben spoke the words as though trying to make himself believe them.

"Not a girl, really," Miss Bullard answered. "Aunt Em is an elderly lady, or a woman at least."

He still stared at the papers in his hands. "Of course, with makeup and costuming, Ben, there's no reason why a talented young man couldn't play the part."

"You want me to play Aunt Em," he stated flatly. *What kind of woman is this?* he asked. *What's she doing, playing some kind of sick joke on me? Is this some kind of initiation? She can't really expect me to play somebody's aunt!*

"It's up to you, Ben. I'm just telling you what's available. There are other parts, of course, in the chorus and maybe something small, here or there. You're certainly welcome to one of those. But you're also welcome to read the part of Aunt Em."

Ben thought of Randi.

This isn't exactly what I had in mind, he reasoned. *She's probably not going to be impressed about having a boyfriend who wears a dress in front of the whole school.*

He glanced up at Miss Bullard, who watched him, waiting patiently, still smiling that same smile.

But I will be in the drama club, at least. And I'll even have a major part my first time around. Of course, I won't want to tell Randi I just joined, so she can't know it's my first time. Still, he argued, *it's something.*

"I guess I can give it a try," he told Miss Bullard. He looked down again at the papers in his hands. "Where did you say to start reading?"

Miss Bullard pointed once more to the line she had first told him to read.

"I'll read Dorothy's part," she instructed. *That's right*, Ben realized. *Playing the part of Em will mean I'll have to spend some time going over lines with Angie. That shouldn't be too hard to take. He reached up with a hand and combed his hair quickly with his fingers.*

With a start he realized that Miss Bullard had already read her line and was waiting for "Aunt Em." He gave her a guilty look.

"I'm sorry. Can you start again? I guess I wasn't quite ready."

"Aunt Em," Miss Bullard squealed, "just listen to what Miss Gulch did to Toto!"

Ben cleared his throat hastily.

"Dorothy, please, we're trying to count."

Miss Bullard immediately placed a hand gently on his shoulder.

"You're AUNT Em, Ben, not UNCLE Em. Can you read it again and try to sound like a silver-haired farm woman?"

"Oh," Ben replied, thinking suddenly. *This might not be as easy as I thought. I gotta talk like a woman, too?*

He cleared his throat again. Miss Bullard repeated Dorothy's line.

"Dorothy, please," he pronounced in falsetto, "we're trying to count."

"Skip the next couple lines, now, to where Dorothy says: 'Oh, the poor little things. Oh, but Aunt Em, Miss Gulch hit Toto right over the back with a rake just because she says he gets into her garden and chases her nasty old cat every day.' "

Ben smiled as Miss Bullard spoke the lines, imagining red-haired Angie saying the words.

"Seventy." It was his line now. "Dorothy, please."

"Oh, but he doesn't do it every day. Just once or twice a week, and he can't catch her old cat anyway. She says she's going to get the sheriff and . . ."

"Dorothy," Ben's falsetto broke in. "Dorothy, we're busy."

"Excellent!" said Miss Bullard, dropping the script on the desk. "Your timing was very good right there. A lot of people really have to work on that, but you jumped right in. And the voice will come, too, with time."

"Thanks," Ben said, still in falsetto. "Er, I mean, thanks," he repeated, dropping his voice an octave.

Miss Bullard proceeded to hand him some photocopied pages of schedules and rules and tips and "miscellaneous info." He gathered them into a stack, straightened the edges on the desk top and mumbled a goodbye as he left the room.

I guess I should be pleased with myself, he thought. *After all, I accomplished an awful lot today. A lot more than yesterday, that's for sure,* he reflected, remembering his efforts to break into the Circle.

Still . . . He interrupted his train of thought while he fiddled with the combination to his locker door and pulled out his homework and makeup work for tonight. *I'm playing an old lady, for crying out loud!*

He closed the locker and headed out the glass doors of the school.

The drama club's a major step, he thought as he walked toward home. *A step in the right direction. The question now is, will it be enough?*

Chapter 16

$\mathcal{B}$en sat upright at the sound of the jangling phone. "Man," he said, "I never realized how that sound comes right through the walls."

He pushed his chair back from his desk which was strewn with the havoc of a month's worth of makeup work, a weekend's worth of homework and a few remnants from that morning's Sunday school class, which again had shown Ben's lack of preparation. He jumped through his bedroom door and peered toward the telephone table.

His father had answered it and now stood extending the receiver an arm's length in Ben's direction as a silent beckoning.

Ben hurried across the room and grabbed the phone. "Thanks," he said, as his father resumed his position on the couch.

Ben spoke into the phone. Randi's voice answered.

"We didn't get much chance to talk today," she started, "so I thought I'd call. Whatcha doing?"

"Just homework," he answered. *Seems like that's all*

I ever do anymore, he thought.

Silence followed Ben's short response. He swallowed, trying to think of something to say quickly. His mind had been so occupied with his salvage efforts at school that lately he was at a loss for what to say when he spoke with Randi.

Randi broke the silence. "I thought maybe we could talk about tomorrow some. It is the 'big day,' you know."

"Yeah," Ben said. Panic gripped him. He felt like he was hovering over the room watching himself sit there in stupid silence. He felt as if he wasn't in his body. He wanted to grab himself by the shoulders and shake himself. He felt this other self say to the statue of his body, *TALK to her, you jerk! What are you doing? SAY something!*

Randi broke the silence again. "I guess you're too busy right now, though, huh?" She was trying to control herself, but her irritation or hurt or whatever it was surfaced in her voice.

"No," Ben started, but he faltered again and silence gripped the phone line once more. After a few moments of icy stillness in the conversation, he stammered out, "Well, I guess I do have a lot of homework."

"Yeah," Randi said crisply. "I shouldn't have bothered you." He started to interrupt, but she continued, "I'll see you tomorrow." She hung up.

He sat, unmoving, with the receiver at his ear until her click was followed by another which, in turn, was followed by the dial tone.

He hung up the receiver and sat stone-faced.

Methodically he rose from the chair, plodded into his room, turned off the light and undressed in the dark. He couldn't bear to risk accidentally catching a glimpse of himself in the mirror.

*****

Monday morning dawned with a beauty that mocked Ben's misery.

He planned to arrive at school early, intending to squirrel his freshman textbooks away in his locker before meeting Randi in front to escort her to her homeroom. He succeeded in dragging his father out of the trailer a few minutes earlier than usual, but had to sit fuming in the car while they waited for a train at the Reading Road crossing. He arrived at school as the bell was ringing. He searched the scurrying crowd of students, but Randi was nowhere in sight.

Panicked prayer occupied the brief homeroom period.

"Lord," he said, not so much speaking as mouthing the words, "I know I've been really busy lately with homework and stuff and haven't really spent much time with You or anything, but PLEASE, You've seen how hard I've been trying to make this work and I really have sort of gotten back on track as far as school goes and You know I've done everything I possibly can, so PLEASE, PLEASE, help me out today, help me out this week, will You? Just give me a little help and I promise I'll show this school what a real Christian is."

The bell forestalled any more promises on Ben's part, but he rose from his desk ready to carry his elaborate "Project AWOL" through to completion.

First period was barely underway when, just as Mr. Billups tossed his attendance book onto the desk after taking roll, a mighty sound pierced the air.

Fire Alarm!

Billups, his voice loud over the din of the alarm, issued directions to the class. Notebooks were slammed shut. Girls clutched their purses in a death-grip. Lights were turned out. Windows were closed. Guys cracked stupid jokes about the supposed fire. Billups barked more instructions.

Ben shuffled with the group, down the hall, to the back stairs, down and out on the lawn away from the building.

Teachers clumped in groups of three or four while the students stood in loose lines. As he waited near the rear of the line, Ben reflected that it was at times like these that the freshmen he spent the school day with seemed most immature. He watched them condescendingly and then raised his eyes to look around him at the other classes lined up in ragged rows like checkout lines at the grocery store.

That's when he saw her.

Randi stood just two lines away, her chin raised into the air scanning the crowd like Ben was doing.

He started to wave a hand at her to capture her attention, when he realized—*I'm standing in line with a bunch of freshmen. If she sees me, she might wonder why, she might even make the connection with Billups and biology and . . . and I can't let her see me!*

He whirled, turning his back toward Randi, and then peeked back over his shoulder to see if she had seen him.

Stupid! he chided himself. *You've got to get out of sight.*

He stooped, like a soldier running across an open field under artillery fire, and ducked behind those ahead of him in line, placing their bodies between himself and Randi. In doing so, however, he found that he drew their attention to him and they turned to look at him and wonder out loud what he was doing.

Help! I've got to get away. Frantically, he dashed for one of the modern sculptures that dotted the lawn, gifts of "the class of" this year or that. It was only a few yards from the end of his line, and once behind it, he imagined he could safely conceal himself until the lines filtered back into the building.

I should be able to catch up with the rest of the class before they even make it back to the room, he calculated.

He had just reached the longed-for safety of the sculpture when Billups nailed him. "AWOL!" he shouted.

Ben froze in his tracks, then turned around slowly.

"AWOL," Billups boomed, loud enough for the whole school to hear. "What are you doing?"

Ben lifted his hand to shield the side of his face from Randi's view as he turned and shrugged. He strode quickly to his place in line, wanting desperately to peek at Randi to see if she'd recognized him but fearing that to do so would mean certain discovery.

My only chance of getting out of this, he figured, *is to keep my face hidden and hope that Randi didn't recognize me.*

The school bell rang finally, and the students began to stream back into the building. Ben kept his hand at his head until he was inside the doors.

Randi occupied his thoughts for the rest of first period.

Maybe she didn't recognize me. After all, Billups didn't call me by name, did he? He thought hard. *No, he said "AWOL." Didn't he? Yeah, that's right. It's possible that Randi didn't make the connection, that she didn't pay any attention.*

He was still brooding on the morning's events in second period and into third period.

Matter of fact, he decided, *I should be grateful that I didn't get to walk Randi to homeroom this morning.* His eyes widened at the full realization of what that had come to mean. *Yeeaah,* he thought. *She hasn't seen me yet today, so she doesn't know what I'm wearing!* He held his hands out from his body and inspected his clothes. *She probably didn't recognize me!*

He lifted his eyes heavenward in a sincere gesture of thanks to God.

Of course . . . He felt a thought brewing inside his head. He sat breathless, oblivious to the action of the teacher or his classmates around him. Finally, the thought was full-blown. *That means I can't let her see me for the rest of the day. I've still got a chance as long as she doesn't see me before I can change my clothes.*

He was suddenly aware of a stillness in the room that hadn't been there before. He raised his head and looked around. Everyone was looking at him. Confusion gripped him.

"Miss Hoffman just called you up to her desk,"

explained the short, curly-headed kid next to him.

"No, she didn't," Ben answered, unbelieving. "Seriously?"

The boy rolled his eyes and shrugged his shoulders.

Ben looked at the teacher. She bent over her desk, writing. Ben sat frozen to his chair. Finally, she lifted her head.

"Ben?" She extended a piece of paper to him.

He jumped from his chair and went to the desk.

"You know who Miss Black is, don't you?"

He hesitated.

"Uh, yeah, sure," he lied. He took the piece of paper and slithered out of the room. He paused a few steps down the hall and, with a glance in each direction, opened the loosely-folded note.

Determining that it was a request for some equipment or supplies, he hastily refolded it and set out for the school office.

"If I'm wrong," he mumbled to himself, "they can at least tell me who Miss Black is."

He had just rounded the corner when, at the opposite end of this wing and walking briskly in his direction, Randi's thin figure came into view. Ben panicked.

She'll see me! She'll see what I'm wearing.

He stepped back around the corner, his breath coming in gasps.

I'll just run down this hall to the staircase at the other end. Rats! A teacher was walking his direction from that end of the hall. *With my luck,* he mourned, *she'd stop me and say, "Now go back to where you started running and show me that you know how to walk,"* and *end up humiliating me in front of Randi.*

He peeked back around the corner. Randi was just yards away.

He cast about frantically for someplace to go, someplace to hide.

The boy's room, he thought, then dismissed it quickly. It was around the corner in the part of the hallway Randi was in.

Desperately, he scrutinized his surroundings.

That's her! I can hear her steps. She's almost here!

Ben spied a door across the hall with a long rectangular window in it. He leaped to the door, flung it open, stepped in, turned and closed it behind him.

He peered through the tall window in the door, waiting for Randi to pass. His attention was arrested, however, by sounds behind him. He turned, first his head, then his shoulders, then the rest of his body.

He had jumped into a class in session.

The students gaped at him with wide eyes and open mouths. The teacher seemed to be holding her place by pointing her finger on the page of the textbook in her hands. She, too, stared at Ben.

Ben felt his face start to flush.

He rapidly debated his options. He could leap back out the door and pray that Randi had passed, and hope that the teacher would resume her teaching and let him escape unpunished. He could apologize, explain that he got confused and walked into the wrong room and ask the teacher's forgiveness.

Instantly, the solution hit him. Bracing himself, he strode confidently to the lady holding the book. He extended the folded note in his hand to her. She shot

Ben a puzzled look and took the note, unfolded it and read it.

"This note is for Miss Black," she said.

Ben was ready for that and was prepared with his answer as if he had rehearsed it all morning.

"It is?"

"Yes, it's a note from Miss Hoffman to Miss Black. Why are you bringing it to me?"

"Well," he said, feigning surprise, "I don't know. I just came from Miss Black." Then he paused as if thinking. "She must have given me the wrong note." He reached out his hand for the note.

The teacher folded it again and returned it to Ben.

"I'm sorry," he said, and she turned to the class and resumed her lesson.

Ben left the room carefully. Randi was gone. He closed the door gently behind him and strode proudly down the hall toward the office again.

After a performance like that, he told himself, *Aunt Em should be a piece of cake.*

Chapter 17

Ben pulled Charlie aside between lunch periods. Charlie greeted him enthusiastically.

"AWOL, man, that was hoot this morning when Billups nailed you during the fire drill," Charlie said.

"You saw it, huh?"

"Yeah," he answered, smiling broadly. Suddenly his smile disappeared and expression was serious. "Did Randi?"

"I don't know, Charlie, that's why I made sure I got to you before you got in the lunch line." He explained the further events of the morning, and the reason he didn't want to take the chance of Randi seeing him in the same clothes he wore during the fire drill.

"So what are you going to do?" Charlie asked. "Go home and change or something?"

Ben shook his head from side to side and grasped Charlie's elbow, leading him away from the cafeteria. Glancing nervously around for sight of Randi, like a spy checking to see if he's followed, he led Charlie to the door of the boys' room.

"In here," he whispered, with one last look around before they entered.

Once inside, they faced each other before the row of sinks and mirrors.

"Change shirts with me," Ben said. He slid his three-button shirt over his head, raising his hair into a ridiculous crown.

Charlie stared at the bare-chested Ben. He fidgeted, conscious of the strange looks he and Ben were receiving from the steady stream of guys flowing by them.

Ben was holding his shirt toward Charlie.

"C'mon, Charlie, give me a hand," he said impatiently.

Some of the junior and seniors were making slightly off-color suggestions at the pair.

They still faced each other, flushing with embarrassment.

"Okay," he said finally, "but just the shirt. No pants or anything like that." He started to lift his T-shirt over his head.

"Give me a break," Ben said sarcastically. "We're both wearing jeans. What good would switching pants do?"

They traded shirts, Charlie putting on Ben's three-button shirt and Ben donning Charlie's T-shirt. As they stood face to face, tucking the shirts into their jeans, the crowd of eight or nine observers cackled and heckled mercilessly, until the two friends raced out of the boys' room and the door shut on the ridicule the group threw at them.

"Thanks, Charlie," Ben said seriously.

Charlie still wore the red flush of embarrassment,

but he managed a shrug. They entered the cafeteria together.

"Don't you have a class this period?" Charlie asked Ben.

"Yeah, but I'm late anyway, so I figured I'd try to find Randi for a second. A few minutes won't make much difference. Late is late."

They stood shoulder-to-shoulder just inside the door for a few moments, scanning the noisy lunch crowd. Charlie elbowed his friend and pointed.

"There she is."

Ben followed the direction of his friend's pointed finger until he picked Randi out of a row of female heads on the far side of the cafeteria. He started in that direction, tossing a few words of parting back over his shoulder at Charlie.

There was no room to take a seat next to Randi, so Ben stationed himself behind her, leaned forward with both hands on his knees, and spoke into her ear.

"Hi," he said, with heartfelt conviction.

She turned, a few strands of her hair brushing Ben's mouth.

"Hi," she returned.

"How's it going so far?"

"Okay, I guess."

"I'm sorry I haven't seen you before this," he said. "I planned to get here early this morning to walk you to your homeroom, but we got held up by a train."

She shrugged easily.

Then, like a swimmer testing the water with a toe, he tried, "I saw you during the fire drill in first period." He braced himself with his shaking knees.

"Did you see me?"

"No," she said innocently. "I looked for you, though."

Ben's chest relaxed with an immense sigh.

"Well," he said, "I better get to class. Want to meet out front to walk home together after school?"

She nodded her head cheerfully.

"Great," he said. "Meet me at the flagpole, okay?"

She agreed, and he felt the urge to kiss her there but, afraid she'd be embarrassed, he simply smiled at her and turned toward the cafeteria exit.

Once around the corner and out of sight of the cafeteria, Ben pumped his fist in the air. "All right," he muttered under his breath.

He hustled to his class with a feeling of victory and accomplishment rising in his chest. He'd weathered the storms of the morning: the train that made him late, the fire drill fiasco, the close encounter in the hallway, and the tense situation in the classroom. And he did it all without Randi knowing anything was up.

The rest of the afternoon dragged by drearily. He occupied some of it by mentally compiling a list of the various steps in Project AWOL, carefully checking off those he'd completed and noting things that remained unfinished.

Classes: I've attended seven straight days of school (eight, counting today) without missing a class. That's got to be some kind of record for me.

Homework: I'm keeping up pretty well, and making progress with the makeup work, but that's still got a long way to go. Make a note of that, he told himself, *makeup work still needs to be caught up.*

Of course, I'm still in freshman classes and the first lunch period, but I don't suppose there's anything I can do about that.

"The Circle," well, that kinda remains to be seen, but the next meeting's tomorrow and maybe by the time Randi meets any of those guys they'll have accepted me. That one still needs attention, but it shouldn't be a problem.

Drama club is a cinch. I'd rather be playing Scarecrow or Tin Man or something like that, but at least I'm in a club. That ought to count for something.

He reviewed his mental checklist several times during the afternoon, and with each going-over became more confident that he could make it work, that Project AWOL had more than a chance. It could succeed with just one or two breaks and a little more time.

At the sound of the last bell, Ben raced out the classroom door, descended the steps in three leaps, raided his locker like a bandit rifling a safe and appeared at the flagpole to meet Randi all before some students had left their desks.

He paced impatiently until, after it seemed the whole school had streamed out the doors, Randi appeared, hugging books against her chest like someone trying to stay warm. He waved to her and she soon threaded her way to his side.

"Like your classes?" he asked as he took her books and balanced them in one arm, wrapping the other around her slender waist.

"Yeah," she said.

She hesitated in a way that made Ben ask, "But?"

"I just can't believe we're not in any classes together.

I mean, I didn't expect to be in *all* your classes, but you'd think I'd at least get to see you during the day."

"Yeah," Ben said, and shrugged. They walked in silence for a few moments. He held tighter to Randi's waist, uncomfortable at the turn the conversation had taken. After a while, he broke the silence. "At least we can walk home together."

She turned suddenly, breaking his grasp on her.

"I know what!" she said. "Today was only my first day. Maybe I can switch a class or two. Maybe I can see my counselor and work something out."

He started to wrinkle his face and was trying to work out some reasonable objection when Randi said, "Let me see your schedule."

"No!" The word was out before he could change its harshness. He wished he could get it back, especially as he saw the shock, then hurt, register on Randi's face.

"No, Randi," he started, "I didn't mean to say it like that. I'm sorry."

Tears welled up in Randi's eyes.

"Randi, c'mon, I . . . it's just that . . ."

She turned her reddening eyes and furrowed brow to face him. They stood on the sidewalk a few houses away from Randi's new home. Her face twitched with emotion as she fought for control.

"What is it, Ben? What's wrong?"

He looked at her, speechless.

"What is it?" she repeated. "The last couple of weeks you've been, well, you've been different. You've barely called me at all. And when you do call, you talk for a few minutes and then say you've got to go."

He shook his head and opened his mouth.

"No," she continued, "don't try to tell me nothing's wrong, because I know you, Ben Howard. I can tell you haven't been yourself."

Her voice began to get higher, straining with emotion.

"And when I told you that I'd be moving closer, that we'd be going to the same school, I don't know, I guess I expected you to shout or dance or something, but you didn't. In fact, ever since that night, it's been like you don't have time for me, like you don't want to talk to me, like you don't want to see me. Like . . ." Her voice choked off for a moment, but she found it again. "Like you don't want me in any of your classes. Like you don't care anymore. Like you're losing interest in me." She gazed at him with a wounded look.

"Is that what it is, Ben? Because if it is, you should just tell me. You should just tell me. You shouldn't lead me on."

Her voice trailed off, but still she examined Ben. He looked into her eyes, but they were now so clouded that he wasn't sure she was seeing him anymore.

He opened his mouth to speak, but nothing came out immediately. Throughout Randi's tearful monologue, things were churning deep in his gut. He had been struggling night and day to save his relationship with Randi and his efforts had made her feel like he was losing interest.

But how can I explain? I can't make her understand the real situation without admitting to her that I've been lying to her all along.

Randi still gazed at him. Her eyes had cleared slightly, but her face seemed to grow redder with each passing second of silence. Ben seemed incapable of speaking.

While he was still forming in his brain the words he wanted to say, Randi fumbled furiously at her books, pulled them from his grasp and hugged them to herself. She whirled quickly and ran to her house. She climbed the steps with her head down, opened the screen door and then the inside door. She slammed the inside door behind her.

Ben watched in numb silence.

A moment later, the screen door swung closed and gently latched. Ben heard the dull click.

Chapter 18

He stood transfixed on the sidewalk in front of Randi's house, wearing the same numb expression as he had during the tragic conversation with Randi.

The same mind that had functioned so creatively this morning, getting him out of bad situations, now seemed to desert him when he needed it most.

He stared at Randi's house, standing silent and deathly unresponsive since the last metallic click of the closing screen door.

He felt an emptiness in the pit of his stomach, but it wasn't hunger.

This is how it must feel, he reflected, *when someone drugs you.* Everything around him—the trees, the street, the houses—seemed unreal, unrelated to him. He felt like he should be moving, like he should be running after Randi and catching her before she reached the door, calming her, saying to her, "No, Randi, don't run away. Don't go. Don't leave me. Don't ever go." But it was as if the connection from his brain to his arms and legs and mouth had somehow been severed, like a telephone line that suddenly goes dead.

At last, however, Ben turned and began walking, slowly, as if someone else was in control of his legs. He walked toward Spring Park without really deciding that was where he was going. He simply discovered, somewhere along the way, that was his destination.

As he plodded along, the control of his body and mind seemed to return to him, like when feeling returns to a limb that's been asleep. His mind seemed to clear as he walked, and his pace quickened, until he arrived at Spring Park, running, racing, pounding, heaving and gasping for air. He pitched himself onto a grassy slope that dipped into the pond and lay there, panting and groaning loudly, unaware and uncaring if anything or anyone could hear.

"Oh, God," he groaned, his face buried in the grass. "Oh, God," he repeated as he rolled onto his back. Some brown and red leaves clung to his clothes and rolled with him. His limbs flopped out into a spread-eagle position. He spoke into the air, into the grayish blue vastness of the sky.

"God, it's all falling apart so fast." He closed his eyes and had the sensation that the world was spinning beneath him. He opened his eyes again and the sensation subsided.

"It's falling apart so fast." The lazy clouds drifting across his vision seemed to strike a sleepy note somewhere deep inside him.

"I really thought I'd made it," he said. "I thought it

was going to work." The clouds floated on, heedless of his speech.

"And I really thought You were going to help me, Lord." The blunt numbness inside him started to sharpen into anger.

"I really trusted You to help me through this, Lord," he said through gritted teeth and misty eyes. "I *believed*, God, I believed You were going to make the plan work.

"Like this morning, when I was late and I thought it was a bad thing, but it turned out good because of the fire drill, because Randi would've seen my clothes if I'd been on time and might have recognized me when Billups yelled at me. I thought that was You; I thought that was a sign that You were on my side, that You were going to help me." Ben paused. He was aware of a thought, something buzzing around in his head, like a pesky mosquito. He waited for a second, but it fled, and he shook his head as he would shake off an insect.

"And then when I saw Randi in the hall, and I looked every direction but there was no way out—and then I found a way out."

Suddenly, the thought landed and bit into his brain. He sat up suddenly in the grass and crossed his legs. He stared in the direction of the pond. His mouth hung open as though he had to relax his jaw muscles in order to work his brain.

His face turned scarlet and his shoulders sagged. He stopped speaking. His communication turned inward upon himself.

What a jerk I've been. The tiredness, which had disappeared in his anger, returned. He rolled the idea around in his head, turning it, testing it. He saw the message clearly now. *I've been asking God's help when, all along, the plan was wrong.*

I should have realized it when I had to go on lying to Dad and Randi and everybody.

He thought back over the last two weeks.

Man, how could I have been so stupid? I was trying to build an image as a Christian student by doing completely un-Christlike things. I guess I've gotten so good at lying to everybody that I didn't even realize what I was doing. I bet not even an hour went by from the time I asked God for help until I lied to that teacher about why I burst into her class.

He stood, brushed himself off and started to stroll around the pond. He looked down at his shirt again. It wasn't even his shirt, it was Charlie's. He thought back over the other events of the day. It seemed as if it had been someone else, not him, who had switched shirts with his friend and then went to meet Randi in disguise.

Man, he thought, *my whole plan was just one big lie from beginning to end. I can't believe it! I was asking God to help me lie to Randi, to make her believe things about me that weren't true.*

He stooped and picked up a handful of pebbles from the ground.

So what are you going to do? he asked himself.

He swallowed hard and tossed a pebble into the pond. He watched the ripples pulse across the surface.

He threw another pebble, unwilling to answer his own question.

If I tell her the truth . . .

His eyes clouded. His throat tightened. *If I tell her the truth,* he repeated, *I'll lose her.*

He rattled the pebbles in his cupped hand. *Of course, she's bound to find out anyway. I can't keep up this stupid lie all year. Even if I could, I might end up losing her because she thinks I'm losing interest in her.* He smiled mirthlessly. *That's a laugh! If she only knew the truth.*

He tossed another pebble into the smooth surface of the water.

And what's the difference? If I tell her the truth, she's going to drop me like a lead weight. If I don't tell her, I stand to lose her anyway.

He lobbed another stone into a placid place in the pond.

I guess if I'm going to lose her, I'd rather lose her because of the truth than because of a lie.

He flung the rest of the pebbles, cutting the water with a dozen tiny explosions. As the ripples fanned out, colliding with each other until they disappeared, Ben turned and walked away.

He arrived at Randi's house as they were eating dinner. Mrs. White invited him to join them, but Ben refused politely and said he'd simply come back in a little while. He realized that he hadn't eaten dinner—he hadn't even been home since school let out—but food seemed unimportant right now.

He turned down the street and walked until he could no longer see the house with the wide porch. He squatted and sat on the curb, his elbows resting on his knees and his arms jutting out into the street.

As he sat, he rehearsed what he would say to Randi.

He tried to make it sound noble, or at least reasonable. When that didn't work, he adapted the posture of a victim, to make it seem like what had happened wasn't his fault. No matter how he phrased it, though, he couldn't make it sound like the truth.

With a glance at his watch, he determined that enough time had elapsed and he couldn't put this off any longer. He rose and retraced his steps to Randi's porch, aware as he walked that the evening had begun to turn cold.

He rang the doorbell. Randi answered. She stepped back in the doorway and invited him in.

He didn't move.

"Can we talk?" he said, pitching his head toward the steps behind him. "Out here?"

She stepped out onto the porch and started to sit beside him on the top step.

"I'm going to get a sweater," she said as she straightened herself above him. "Be right back."

He waited alone on the steps, in the same posture as on the curb. A moment later she returned and sat, her long legs stretched across the steps in front of her. She leaned lightly against Ben's arm.

They sat together in the darkening silence, neither of them speaking. They heard the door open behind them. They turned and saw Pastor White's form framed by the screen door. He closed the door slowly. A moment later, the porch light came on.

Ben struggled within himself to begin, but failed at his first several attempts.

"Randi," he said finally, not looking at her but staring out into the street. "I don't know how to start this." He stopped and cleared his throat. *Amazing how fast your throat can dry up on you,* he thought.

"But I want you to listen to everything I've got to say before you say anything."

He looked at her. She was studying his face. He held her gaze for a moment, then looked away from her eyes. He searched for some way to begin, but the words would not form in his mind. Finally, the silence became unbearable to him.

"They call me 'AWOL'," he began abruptly, then went on, rapidly reciting every detail of the last two years, starting from before the time they had started dating. He told her about skipping school and forging phony absence excuses. He told her about intercepting the school's phone calls to his dad and about impersonating his father on the phone. He confessed to her about all the classes he'd flunked and how he was still a freshman. He told her about his reputation as a junkie at school. He told her how, many times, he'd determined to go back to school and get back on track, but how he'd failed or given up each time.

The door opened again and Pastor White traversed the porch to the mailbox near where Ben and Randi sat. He opened it, peeked in and then closed it again with a shrug. He entered the house once more.

Ben waited a moment. Then, as Randi sometimes looked at him, sometimes looked down at the steps and sometimes looked out into the street, he reviewed the events of the last two weeks: how he felt when she told him her news at Mama's Pizza; his depression and feeling that their relationship was over; the development of Project AWOL, the classes, the makeup work, the Circle, the drama club, and the harrowing events of this morning and afternoon.

He stopped. He felt like he shouldn't be stopping, that he should be saying something more, that he should begin to plead with her, to tell her he loved her, to say to her, "Please don't drop me." But the feeling he'd had on the walk home earlier this afternoon overwhelmed him again. He had said all he could say. Nothing else would come out.

The door opened behind them once more. Randi's father came outside and walked around to the side of the house, leaving them sitting in silence. He reappeared a moment later with a leaf rake in his hand and began raking the few leaves that dotted the lawn in front of Ben and Randi.

Ben looked at her dumbly. His eyes welled with tears.

She is so beautiful, he thought. He watched her. She looked at him, then glanced away into the street. He tried to read her expression. He struggled to guess her thoughts. He fastened his eyes on her.

Randi turned her face away from Ben. He stared devotedly at the back of her head, waiting for her to meet his gaze again.

She sat in that position for what seemed an eternity.

Please, God, he prayed, *don't let her yell; don't let her hate me.*

Pastor White collected the leaves into a small pile several feet from the couple. He carried the rake onto the porch, propped it against the house and went back inside.

Finally Randi turned her head. She dropped her

144

chin to her chest for a moment and stared at the porch step beneath her feet. Then she raised red eyes and tear-streamed cheeks to Ben and took a slow, deep breath, preparing to speak.

Ben knew what she was going to say.

"How could you lie to me?"

or

"How can I ever trust you or believe in you again?"

or

"How can you call yourself a Christian?"

She looked at him and finally, seriously, her voice higher than usual, she said, "You really did all that for me?"

Ben looked at her, hang-mouthed, and said, "What?"

"I mean, you really did all that for me? You went back to school after *two years* and did all that you've done the last two weeks because you didn't want to lose me?"

Ben summoned all his eloquence for his answer.

"Uh huh."

She flung her arms around his neck and, after a moment of shocked stillness, he wrapped her tightly in his arms.

The door opened again. The tearful couple unwrapped themselves awkwardly as Pastor White came outside with a plastic garbage bag. Ben and Randi watched happily as he raked the tiny collection of leaves into the bag.

Chapter 19

$\mathcal{B}$en paced the narrow hall outside Pastor White's study. He rubbed his palms against his jeans and ran his tongue over his lips.

This is the worst, he told himself. He whirled in front of the potted palm at the end of the hall and sulked back toward the low twin tables that stood like sentinels outside the pastor's door. *I don't think I can do it,* he thought.

He stared at the pastor's door as if he expected a hideous monster to break through at any moment and attack him ferociously. He swallowed and raised his fist as if to knock on the door.

He had not foreseen this two days ago when he had agreed to let Randi tell her father about their conversation on the porch. As he thought about it now, he didn't remember what response he had expected, but he sure hadn't expected the man to call him at home and ask him to come down to the church on a Saturday to meet with him.

Ben's hand floated in mid-air. He couldn't bring

himself to knock on the door. He felt feverish.

I can't do it, he decided. *I'll call him from home and tell him I didn't feel well.* He opened his hand and rubbed his clammy forehead. *At least I won't be lying*, he thought. He turned suddenly, determined to make a quiet escape, when his left knee banged into the little table.

The blow propelled the only object on the table—a small leafy plant in a clay pot—onto the floor with a scrape and a crash that echoed in the hall like a train roaring through a tunnel.

Ben froze for a moment of indecision, wondering whether to make a mad dash down the hall or stay and face the pastor. *Get out, get out*, his heart seemed to beat in rapid rhythm. *Run for it*, he commanded his feet. But in the same second, he told himself, *No, Pastor will come through that door any second and he'll see you running away like a criminal.* No sooner had the thought crossed his mind than the door flew open and Pastor White stood beside him.

"Are you all right?" the pastor asked.

Ben nodded, and stammered a clumsy apology.

They stood side by side, surveying the scene. Wordlessly, Pastor White ducked into his study and returned a moment later with a small wastebasket. He knelt on the floor and began sweeping up dirt and broken pieces of pot with his hands. Ben watched him, awkwardly, and finally knelt beside him to help.

When they had transferred most of the mess to the wastebasket, Pastor White turned to Ben. "That'll do for now. I have a little chore to do this morning. I'd like you to come along if you don't mind."

Ben began to entertain visions of gloom and doom, one after the other. *Maybe he's taking me to a mental hospital to get me away from his daughter. Maybe he's taking me to a secluded spot where he can throw me off a cliff.* He shook his head at his own stupidity. *Nah, he'll probably just take me out for a Big Mac and tell me he doesn't think Randi and I should keep seeing each other. He'll probably call it "taking a break from each other," or something like that.*

He followed the pastor to his car, a blue minivan. They sat silently as Pastor White steered out of the church parking lot and headed north, away from town.

They passed through the tree-lined streets of the north side of town, and turned left at the Crestview Golf Course. They continued for several miles until they were surrounded by farmland. They spoke little, though Pastor White occasionally looked over at Ben and smiled wisely.

After what seemed an eternity to Ben, the car slowed, turned into a long driveway, and stopped in front of a large white farmhouse. Pastor White signaled Ben to accompany him up the walk to the house, and they stood shoulder to shoulder before the door. The pastor raised a fist and knocked loudly on the door.

An elderly woman answered the door.

"We're here to cut your wood for you, Mrs. Sharp," the pastor said.

The woman cast a questioning glance at Ben, and the pastor introduced him. Ben smiled and nodded at the woman.

The pastor and Mrs. Sharp chatted easily for a few moments, until the woman seemed to tire of the conversation and abruptly said, "The chain saw should be in the shed."

Ben followed the pastor down the porch steps as the woman shut the door behind them. They rounded the corner of the house and entered the backyard.

Pastor White ducked into the shed and emerged a few seconds later, brandishing a large orange-and-white chain saw. He set it down on the ground, unscrewed a black cap and conducted a careful inspection.

"Always check the oil," he told Ben. Then he smiled. "I learned that the hard way." He twisted the cap back on. "Always check the oil," he repeated.

He then led Ben across the yard to a large tree that had been felled and divided into six or seven large pieces.

"Ever use a chain saw before?" the pastor asked.

Ben shook his head.

He handed the chain saw to Ben, placing Ben's hands on the handle and the trigger and then wrapping his hands around Ben's.

"It's easy," he told him. "You just put it against the log like this and rub it back and forth, just like a regular saw." Pastor White guided Ben's hands in a sawing motion against the side of the log.

Ben's forehead wrinkled and he looked sideways at the man.

"What's wrong?" Pastor White asked cheerily.

Ben inspected the pastor's expression. Pastor White returned Ben's gaze without blinking or smiling.

"We've got to start it first," Ben said, propping one foot against the log and resting the saw on his thigh.

"Oh. You want to do it *that* way?"

Ben blushed, whether with embarrassment or confusion he wasn't sure. He kept expecting Pastor White to crack a smile, slap him on the back and admit that he was just having a little fun. But the man's face remained humorless.

"How else am I supposed to do it?" he protested. "It'd be stupid to use a chain saw like a regular saw."

Pastor White locked eyes with Ben. "That's what you've been doing in your Christian life."

Ben immediately dropped his gaze to the ground. *Here it comes*, he thought. *I wondered when he'd get around to it.* His heart sank within him as he contemplated the end of his relationship with Randi.

Pastor White stepped closer to Ben. "You see, Ben," he said, "from what my daughter tells me, you've been trying to live a consistent Christian life—at least for the last couple weeks—in your own power. And from what I hear," he said, chuckling, "you've had quite a time of it."

Ben lifted his head. Pastor White was smiling.

He grasped the chain saw and hoisted it off Ben's leg. "What you've been doing is about like slicing this log without starting the chain saw—only harder." He set the saw down on the ground beside the log and draped an arm around Ben's shoulders.

"You see, Ben, you can't live a consistent Christian life in your power. Neither can I. We need power, just like that chain saw needs gas and oil. And our power comes from the Holy Spirit of God."

"But I thought the Holy Spirit came into my life when I first became a Christian," Ben said.

"He did. And He's still there. But *He's* not the one in control—you are. That's why it seems like no matter how hard you try, you can't be the kind of Christian you want to be."

The pair fell silent for a few moments. A wind rustled the branches of the trees in the yard.

"So what do I have to do?" Ben asked.

Pastor White withdrew his arm from Ben's shoulders. He sat on one of the enormous logs.

"Sit down, Ben," he said, motioning for Ben to sit beside him. "First, you confess and repent of any sin on your heart. If there's any sin you can't or won't give up, then forget it, because you can't grab hold of God's fullness if you're still holding on to some of your sin.

"Then you commit yourself fully to Him. Give yourself completely to the Lord, Ben, holding back nothing; determine that you will follow Him no matter what it costs you, no matter where He leads you, no matter what anyone else does."

Ben felt a knot form in his stomach that began pushing its way up his chest and into his throat. The pastor's words awakened a desire in him that seemed to shake him from the inside out.

"Once you've done that, Ben, you then just ask Him to fill you with His Holy Spirit, to take complete control of everything—*every* thing—in your life. And then, every day, you let Him live His holy life in you, and help you develop a habit—a habit that's fed by praying and studying His Word—of trusting Him to live in you, every day, every minute, through His Holy Spirit."

Pastor White was breathless when he finished speaking. He'd been speaking with such fervor and intensity that his face was red from exertion. He inhaled deeply, and looked at Ben with moist eyes.

"What do you say, Ben?" he asked.

Ben returned his gaze. "Yeah," he said. He sat motionless for a few moments until, suddenly, he swung himself off the log, turned and knelt on one knee, using the log as an altar. Pastor White clapped his hands together once and positioned himself beside Ben.

Ben prayed out loud then, pouring out his heart in a flurry of words. He confessed his lying and trickery; he begged God's forgiveness for his poor witness at school. The pastor guided him with comments and questions from time to time, as Ben surrendered his will completely to God, asking Him to take complete control of his life. He asked God to fill him with the Holy Spirit, and help him to start every day with an attitude of devotion to God and trust in His ability to guide him and keep him from sinning.

Finally, Ben stopped, reviewing in his mind everything that he had said. After a long moment of silence, he uttered a soft "Amen."

Ben and the pastor both stood and embraced.

"Thanks, Pastor," Ben said. His eyes were ringed with emotion.

"Now, remember, Ben—it's in the nature of a fire to go out. You've got to feed it and stir it and keep it going every day. And the way you do that is with prayer and Bible study."

Ben nodded.

Pastor White gripped Ben's shoulder tightly, and smiled widely. "I want you and me to get together every Saturday morning for the next few weeks. You may cut more wood or rake more leaves than you like, but it will give me a chance to see how things are going with you."

Ben nodded. They faced each other for a few moments in silence, neither feeling the need to talk. Finally, the pastor stooped and picked up the chain saw.

"Pastor, wait," Ben said. He struggled to form the words he wished to ask. "What about..." He stopped and cleared his throat. "What about me and Randi?"

The man said nothing, but smiled reassuringly. He yanked the chain saw to life, and exchanged a meaningful glance with Ben.

Ben smiled.

Epilogue

$\mathcal{T}$he response thundered in the Verona High School auditorium. As the curtain rang down on the last performance of *The Wizard of Oz*, the crowd of parents and students and friends applauded enthusiastically.

When the curtain rose again, the cast stepped to the edge of the stage. Arms wrapped around each others' shoulders, they smiled and bowed together.

Three mammoth bouquets of roses were carried on stage. The first was presented to redheaded Angie, who played the lead role. The second bouquet was bestowed upon Miss Bullard, who directed the play.

A moment of suspense preceded the presentation of the third bouquet. As the applause for Miss Bullard dwindled, the fragrant roses were ceremoniously awarded to "Aunt Em," the wigged and stockinged matron portrayed by Ben Howard.

The cast reassembled into a straight line once more for final bows. In the middle of the appreciative audience, a single student stood to her feet, clapping.

From behind his heavy makeup, Ben saw Randi stand alone for a moment until, first a few, then the entire auditorium, rose in a standing ovation for the high school drama.

Ben knew the applause was for the whole cast. But he also knew that one person was cheering just for him.